ANYTHING GOES

Death Comes With a Song in Its Heart

Golden Publishing Company – Lakewood, CO
in collaboration with TWB Press – Centennial, CO
2019

Anything Goes
by George S. Naas

Copyright © 2016 Golden Publishing Company

Edited and formatted for publication by Terry Wright at TWB Press – www.twbpress.com

Published by
Golden Publishing Company, Inc.
PO Box 150425
Lakewood, CO 80215
USA

ISBN: 9780970714282

Anything Goes

ON MONDAY, 7 September 2026, the last day of his life, thirty-two-year-old John Nathan Gee Jr. decided to be a thief just as he had been for most of his sorry life. He was one of the derelicts in Denver, living off the kindness of others. At ten minutes after nine in the morning, he hauled his five-foot-nine inch, 120-pound frame into a Seven Eleven. He was in luck. The store clerk was busy selling the only other customer in the store a Power Ball ticket. Cool as a summer salad, he moseyed over to the junk food aisle and stuffed two packages of Twinkies under his filthy shirt. Then he proceeded to the pop dispenser and filled a Big Gulp cup full of diet Coke. Quickly, he drank half of it then refilled it. Lid and straw in place, he strode to the clerk. He was now the only customer in the store.

"There's something wrong with your pop machine," he bitched to the female clerk and set the full cup on the counter. "This pop tastes watered down."

"I'm sorry, sir. I'll have the manager—"

He slammed fifty cents down and yelled, "This is all this piss pop is worth."

The clerk, noticeably upset and afraid of him, said, "Keep your money, sir."

"Damn right I will." As he picked up the last two quarters to his name, one of them fell off the counter and rolled under the safe. The clerk bent over to get it and, as she did, John liked what he saw of her slim body and cute little ass.

Maybe I'll come back sometime when she's getting off duty and rape her.

She retrieved the quarter and handed it to him. "Have a nice day."

He leaned on the counter like James Bond himself. "What do you say we get together and—" Out the corner of his eye he saw a guy outside heading for the door. John stood up straight and grabbed the cup. "Nah, it's cool. Maybe next time." He beat a hasty retreat.

John made his way down the street to his favorite begging location: The Washington Street down ramp off I-70 West. Traffic was lighter than usual. Then he remembered it was Labor Day. "Shit. Nobody is working today," he mumbled. Business would be bad on this corner. Deciding to make the best of it, he set the diet Coke on the traffic light control box then retrieved his cardboard sign he left nightly behind a nearby bush.

After fourteen minutes of standing around being ignored, he remembered his encounter with the store clerk...and the Twinkies. He was reaching for a package under his shirt when a four-door black Mercedes sedan pulled up to the stoplight. The Twinkies would have to wait. He held up the sign: *Please help a homeless vet and God bless.* In reality, John never came closer to the armed services than war movies he'd watched at the Church of the Risen Jesus that gave shelter to him and other homeless men.

He knew he was in luck when the driver lowered the car's window. Excited, he could already taste the rotgut whisky he'd buy from the discount liquor store down the block.

He fake-limped over to the car door, but instead of seeing a fistful of money in the open window, he saw the double barrels of a sawed-off shotgun pointed at him. "What the hell, man?"

The driver pulled the trigger.

John's guts splattered in all directions. Bloody Twinkie wrappers floated aimlessly in the air as if looking for a new home, and birds nesting under the overpass scattered in panicked flight while the booming echo ricocheted off nearby buildings.

The light changed to green. The Mercedes drove over John's body and the cardboard sign then sped off. At 9:25am, John's days as a beggar and a thief were over.

***

ON THE THIRD anniversary of John's murder, the Mercedes pulled into a driveway off Morrison Road at 10645 Whylie Street and drove a quarter mile to the automatic gate in the white brick wall that surrounded an estate. The gate opened and the car drove up a blacktopped driveway to the house. The driver got out and strode to the front door. Using a remote control device, he opened the three-inch thick sliding steel door and stepped through. As the door closed behind him, the *thunk* sounded more like a bank vault door closing than the front door to a house. He stepped into the elevator and rode it up to the second floor. As he got off, he disabled the elevator doors then walked to his desk and turned on his computer, which instantly started blasting out a song on the outdoor speakers: *Anything Goes.*

Things have changed...

He picked up a picture of his wife and daughter and son, kissed it and softly said, as if they could still hear him, "This country is going to bleed, bleed, bleed. They took you away from me, and now they'll know unimaginable grief."

With hatred wrenching his face, he moved to his command center and switched on the perimeter sensors and remote cameras that covered every inch of his property. Amused at his handiwork, he threw the switch that activated the land mines that protected most of the grounds. He got a Coke from the fridge and walked out on the balcony.

Anything Goes echoed throughout the neighborhoods a half mile away.

Nothing to do now except wait for the cops.

***

AT 11:36am ON MONDAY, 3 September 2029, Officer Dave Hinton received a dispatch to 10645 Whylie Street on a disturbance call. He had hoped this Labor Day would be uneventful. As he pulled up to the driveway gates, he heard loud music coming from four outdoor speakers. Surveying the surroundings, he noticed the strange house sat in the middle of a five-acre estate. It resembled the old Alamo, painted white with no windows on the first floor. He noticed a second-floor balcony, a walkout door, and two windows on either side. The place looked impenetrable under the bright sunlight

A black Mercedes was parked in the driveway, so he knew someone was home, but when he pushed the call button on the intercom box, he got no answer.

"Fuck." He climbed out of the patrol car and pushed on the gate that blocked the driveway, but the gate wouldn't open.

The loud music frazzled his nerves.

Keying the radio mike on his collar, he reported to dispatch. "I'll be on foot. Gotta check this out."

Anything Goes

"Do you need backup?"

"Nah, I think it's just a kid playing his stereo full blast."

He had to get in there and convince the homeowner to turn down the music, but the gate with its sharp points along the top wasn't a safe way to get in. However, the white six-foot brick wall that encircled the estate was no problem to climb.

As he walked up the asphalt driveway, he noticed a large three-foot by eight-foot electronic clock on the front porch. In bright red neon numbers against a black background it showed the correct time: *11:54am*. The speakers kept blaring out the song *Anything Goes*. When it got to the end, it started over. No wonder the neighbors were pissed off and called the police.

Dave scampered up the few steps to a massive steel door and rang the bell. No answer. He rang it again and again with the same results. He yelled, "Anybody home?" but quickly guessed his voice couldn't be heard over the loud music. Angst filled his chest as he thought maybe something terrible had happened to the unresponsive homeowner.

With hastened steps, he walked around the house and

discovered it had no back door and no windows. However, he did notice surveillance cameras following him. He stopped in front of a camera. It stopped and remained pointed at him. Feeling kind of creepy, he waved at the camera. "You all right in there?"

Nothing. Now he thought maybe the place might be a meth lab but immediately discounted that idea. Drug dealers would never draw attention to themselves with loud music.

He completed his tour around the house and decided to ring the doorbell again. As he did, a sticky sweet liquid poured down on him from the balcony above, instantly drenching him. "What the fuck?" He backed away from the door, shook his dripping hair, and looked up to see a guy wearing a Darth Vader mask and holding a Coke can.

"What do you want?" His voice sounded mechanical and hollow.

"Turn off that damn music."

"No can do, man. Did you like that Coke I poured on you? It could have been worse. I could have pissed on you."

Sounded like assault on a police officer to Dave. "Get your ass down here. You're under arrest."

"I'll tell you what, you stupid fuck. I don't think I'll let you arrest me. Besides, you won't have any way to take me to the station. See your cop car over there?"

Dave turned to see the cruiser still idling at the gate. "What about it?"

"Better tell it goodbye."

"Huh?"

A horrendous explosion lifted the car a good ten feet into the air. Parts flew from a rolling ball of fire, and the concussion blew down the iron gates.

Dave ducked the fury. His ears rang so badly he could barely hear *Anything Goes*.

The guy looked down at Dave and yelled, "Run, run, run for your shitty life."

Dave couldn't believe what he saw. The guy on the balcony now brandished a big-ass machinegun. It rattled off bullets that spit dirt at his feet. Dave took off running in a zigzag pattern. Adrenaline lit fires in his bloodstream. His heart must've been beating 170 times a minute as he keyed his collar microphone and yelled, "Shots fired. Shots fired. Officer needs backup. Send SWAT."

In less than thirty seconds, he made it to the wall and scrambled over it as white brick dust blew up all around him. He landed in a ditch and lay there in eight inches of water.

"Fuck."

He was shaking uncontrollably. To his right, what was left of his police cruiser lay on its side, the front wheels slowly turning like burnt marshmallows in a raging campfire. Amazingly, the emergency lights were blinking until he heard the rattle of that machinegun cut loose again. Bullets ripped into the cruiser, which soon began to resemble melting Swiss cheese.

A tire exploded.

He pushed his body down deeper into the ditch. When he turned his head, he found himself looking at an ugly brown spider swaying in the breeze on its web. A piece of shrapnel grazed his cheek. "Shit." Head down, he closed his eyes and hoped another piece of steel wouldn't hit him in the skull. When he opened his eyes, the spider web was now in tatters, still waving in the breeze. The shrapnel had hit the spider dead center, cutting it in half. He had no love for spiders but felt sorry for this one.

Wrong place, wrong time, pal.

After a few more seconds, the firing stopped. All he

could hear was the ringing in his ears, the pop and fizz of his police car, and that damn music, *Anything Goes,* only louder.

Dave twisted his body around in the ditch and crawled as fast as he could away from the carnage. He made it to where the ditch met up with Oak Street. There, an old man in his eighties leaned on a walker. "What's all the commotion, son?"

Is this shit for real? Maybe I'm dreaming.

Dave was about to tell the old guy to skedaddle when a police cruiser careened to a halt just three feet from him. Right behind that car came two more. Tire smoke stunk up the air. The place was soon crawling with Lakewood police.

"You guys filmin' a movie?" the old man asked.

"Get out of here, sir." Dave wiped mud from his uniform.

The old man started to push his walker toward Dave's now totally destroyed police cruiser.

"Stop that old bastard," Dave shouted to his backup officers. "Get him out of here and close off the streets."

One policeman stopped the old man. "Which way do you live, sir?"

The old man answered by pointing to the house just

south of their position.

"Then go that way now. You're in the middle of a police investigation."

"More like a standoff," Dave said. "It's not safe around here, sir."

Looking at Dave, the old man squinted. "Better do somethin' about that cut on your face."

"Thanks for the advice."

The old fellow mumbled to himself as he left.

Dave, still shaking from an adrenaline overload and his soaked uniform, felt relieved to see the Lakewood SWAT truck show up. Lt. Ron Peterson, the SWAT team leader, stormed over to Dave. "What do you got? Fill me in."

"We got one crazy bastard on our hands." Dave told him what happened then sat on the SWAT truck bumper and lit up a cigarette. His hair dripped Coke and water. "Whatever happens, he's my collar, got that?"

Lt. Peterson put his hand on Dave's wet shoulder. "We'll get this guy for you. Just take it easy."

That goddamned music was enough to make them all go insane.

One of Peterson's men, loaded down with gear and

guns, rushed up. "We have the place surrounded, sir."

Peterson looked around: Hogback to the west, a new housing development to the east, and an old neighborhood to the north. "Thank God this is an isolated part of the city. Is that one house vacant?" He pointed to the south where a lone house sat among the trees.

"An old man lives there, is all. Nothing else within a half a mile, mostly open ranch land."

He looked at the Alamo. "Do we have a phone number for the asshole in there?"

Before he could get an answer, police headquarters radioed him. "Answer your cell phone when it rings."

Dave took a slow drag on his cigarette. "Probably Darth Vader calling."

"Darth Vader?" Peterson frowned.

"He's wearing a mask...fuckin' crazy, I tell ya."

Within thirty seconds the phone rang. Peterson answered. "Who is this?"

A tinny electronic voice said, "Hey, shit head, put on the cop whose cruiser I just shot up."

"He's not available at the moment."

The mechanical voice roared, "You heard me, you

fucking prick."

Peterson handed Dave the phone. "Tell him to turn off that damn music."

After the near-death experience he'd just gone through, Dave didn't want to talk to the asshole; he wanted to kill him. He wiped blood from his cheek so he wouldn't get it on the phone when he put it up to his ear. "Who the hell are you, anyway?"

"I'm the guy who spared your life. Nice of me, huh? Your wife could be fucking some other prick by now."

"Leave my wife out of this."

"I saved your marriage, man. Do I even get a thank you?"

"How about a fuck you?"

"Oh, you are a bad ass, aren't you?"

Dave huffed. "Just turn off the music."

"What? You don't like my favorite song? *Anything Goes.* Yeah, that's what it's going to be around here from now on. Anything goes."

"What do you want?"

"Maybe I got a parking ticket and it pissed me off."

"What's your name? I'll take care of that ticket for you."

"Ah-ah-ah... You first."

"Officer Dave Hinton. Your turn."

"You can call me Bill, you can call me Ralph, you can call me anything but Rumpelstiltskin."

Dave fought to keep his voice calm. "You're in a world of shit, and you want to make a joke?"

"Well, Dave, the whole world is a fucking joke."

"You must know we've got you surrounded. You can't escape, so the joke's on you, fucker."

"This shithole of a country is the joke, Dave. We're all just jokesters, here to provide God with entertainment. That's our real job, Dave, not playing cops and robbers."

"You're crazier than a whole flock of loony birds."

"Well, you hit the head on the nail."

"Nail on the head, you mean."

"I reversed the words, Dave. Proves I'm not crazy. It's the crazies who were put into that primordial soup eons ago. They spice up our lives. Otherwise, we'd all be bored assholes instead of just plain assholes."

"What kind of asshole are you?"

"Take that cop hiding behind what's left of your police car. Is he an asshole?"

Dave saw Officer Gilmore. "He has a wife and three kids."

"He thinks he's hidden by the smoke, keeps peeking around the fender like he's looking for a clear shot at me. What he doesn't realize is there's a hole through the police car that lines up with his fat gut. I have a perfect bead on him. So I'm going to let you make a command decision, Dave. Do I let him live or do I blow a hole in his donut-filled guts?"

"Don't kill him. That won't prove anything." Dave put his hand over the phone and motioned to a nearby officer. "Get him out of there." He pointed at the cop hunkered down behind the smoldering car.

A shot rang out. The cop writhed on the ground, screaming. Blood spewed from his left knee.

"What the fuck?" Dave yelled into the phone. "You didn't give me a chance to get him out of there."

"Relax, Dave. He isn't going to die. I just cut short his police flag football career. Tell your boys to drag him out of there. I won't shoot at them."

"How do we know you're not lying?"

"Because I never lie, Dave. I'm not a cop or a fucking

politician or a god damn preacher."

As Dave watched two officers run toward the downed cop, he heard the Channel Eight helicopter circling a thousand feet overhead.

Peterson groaned. "It didn't take those news vultures very long to get here."

Dave looked back to see the officers slowly pulling the injured cop out of harm's way. Dave's train of thought was interrupted by a loud bang followed by a deafening roar. The Channel Eight copter spun wildly out of control. Fire and smoke spewed from the cockpit. He heard an officer yell, "My God, he shot it down with a fuckin' missile." Dave screamed into the phone. "You said you wouldn't shoot."

The hollow voice replied in an instant. "I didn't shoot the cops, so what are you bitching about? Besides, I never watch Channel Eight anyway."

"You-you..." Dave's voice cracked. "You just killed people you didn't even know. What's the matter with you?"

"So it's okay to kill people I do know?"

"I don't want you to kill anybody."

"I guess we're past that point, Davey, aren't we. It so happens I did know who was on the helicopter. The traffic reporter is the daughter of Judge Henry Sutton. Or should I say *was*? Now he'll know what it feels like to lose a daughter."

"You'll get the death penalty for this."

Darth Vader laughed. "Dave, I'm going to take a little break for lunch, but you can call me back at *Pennsylvania-six-five-thousand*."

"You're shittin' me. That exchange has been obsolete for decades."

"You remember that song, Dave, from the Glenn Miller collection? God, that tune sure is catchy: *Pennsylvania-six-five-thousand*. Shit! Now it'll be running through my mind for the next week."

"Fuck the nostalgia. You haven't answered my question. What do you want?"

"As Al Jolson once said, "You ain't seen nothing yet."

"Who?"

"Al Jolson was a singer a hundred years ago, back before this country went down the fucking shithole. The time when people had honor and kindness, and the world wasn't run by billionaire assholes. As you'll soon see, Dave, they won't be super rich much longer. You can quote me on that. Meanwhile, don't try anything stupid. You'll find that I might not be so generous if some of those dumb ass cops attempt to take me out. You see, Dave, I have a very unique set of hostages."

"What hostages?"

"I'll let you and the FBI know in an hour."

"We didn't call in the FBI for a nut job like you."

"I know they're on their way so don't try to bullshit me. Maybe they'll bring a forensic shrink with them. I hope the shrink is a woman. You never can tell, Dave, maybe she can get me to give up. Then you boys will be home fucking your wives by dinnertime. The world lives on hope, Davy boy. Goodbye—"

"Wait, wait. Turn off the goddamned music."

The phone clicked dead.

"Shit!"

Lt. Peterson grabbed the phone. "Okay, what's with the asshole? Did he say why he just murdered those people in the helicopter?"

"He said he has hostages."

"Hostages? Who? How many?"

"I don't know."

"Get that asshole back on the line. Now!"

"I can't. He's on his lunch break."

"Lunch break? Are you fuckin' kidding me?"

"He'll call back in an hour."

Peterson's face looked red enough to explode. "I'll make him call back right now." He grabbed a nearby SWAT officer's M-16 rifle and dogged the brick wall until he came to the mangled iron gates. Dave's police car smoldered, and Peterson saw the blood pool left by the wounded policeman. He huffed. "What a fuckin' mess."

Crouched for combat, Peterson took aim at one of the giant speakers and opened fire. Bullets tore through the casing but didn't silence the music until one round hit the wiring. "Ha. One down, three to go."

Before he could line up on the next speaker, all hell broke loose with the *BAM-BAM-BAM* of the machinegun as it chewed big chunks out of the brick wall over his head. He took off running back the way he came, splashing through the water-filled ditch as the rounds followed him and pulverized bricks on top of the wall.

A SWAT team member, perched on the limb of a tree across the street, was just about to zero in on the shooter when he saw the machinegun swivel toward him. "Shit!" He jumped out of the tree a split second before rounds started taking the tree apart. He barely escaped the barrage of bark and splintered wood.

As Peterson got back to the SWAT truck, he saw cops hunkered down behind their cars. He stood bent over and gasping to catch his breath. The phone rang. He answered it and handed it to Dave. "It's for you."

Dave sighed in resignation and took the phone. "Are you going to turn off the music now?"

"Dave..." the mechanical voice said, "Someone just shot the hell out of one of my very expensive speakers. I expect to be reimbursed and hope we can settle this matter out of court like gentlemen."

Peterson, who had been listening over Dave's shoulder, grabbed the phone. "Now listen to me, you fucking prick. If you don't start talking about the hostages, I'll assume you don't have any and order my men to shoot the shit out of your house with you in it."

"So you want to know about the hostages, huh?"

Peterson covered the phone with his hand and looked at Dave. "This guy's not running on all eight cylinders."

Then into the phone: "Don't play games with me."

"Very well. The hostages. I don't have any in the house, however, all of you cocksuckers are my hostages."

Peterson scowled. "Just come out, hands in the air. We'll get you the psychiatric help you need."

"No thanks. You see, boys, I have planted five suitcase-size nuclear bombs all around the country, and I may or may not set them off one at a time or all at the same time. It'll depend on how intelligent you dumb asses are...and, of course, the mood I'm in at the time."

The hair on Peterson's neck prickled. There was no way a civilian could get his hands on enough enriched uranium to build one nuclear bomb, much less five. "I don't believe you."

"I knew you wouldn't, so I'll just have to convince you. When the FBI gets here, put one of them fuckers on the phone. He'll believe me."

Just then, three black SUVs pulled up to the clutch of patrol cars. Doors opened and suited men got out.

Peterson looked at Dave. "Did you call the FBI?"

Dave shook his head. "The fucker must've called the FBI on himself."

Anything Goes

Peterson scratched his head. "This guy's got everything planned down to the split second. He's playin' us big time."

A bald suited man pulled off his sunglasses and stepped up to Peterson. "Special Agent Brad Tillman. What's this I hear about hostages?"

"You're looking at 'em..." Peterson swept a hand to the cops, SWAT officers, and FBI agents. "*We* are the hostages according to this clown." He handed Agent Tillman the phone.

Tillman frowned. "Who is it?"

"Just say hello."

He put the phone to his ear. "This is Agent Brad—"

"Brad, Brad, Brad. Didn't I see your ugly face on TV a while back? I'm sure I did. You arrested the Taco restaurant serial killer."

"Why are you disguising your voice?"

Peterson leaned in. "He thinks he's Darth Vader."

Brad said into the phone. "That was me, but—"

"Great job. I hope they gave you one of those twelve-inch Mexican subs for free."

"What is this all about?"

"So, Brad, you got any family over at the Arches

National Monument in Utah?"

"What game are you playing?"

"This is no game, Brad. In one minute, a large portion of Arches Monument will no longer exist. Hello, hole in the ground!" He laughed.

Tillman looked at Peterson. "What's he talking about?"

"The crazy bastard says he's got five nukes planted around the country. I don't believe him."

"He's lying," Dave put in. "Where's he going to get the stuff to make—"

A porky agent stepped up and whispered into Brad's ear. His face blanched. The agent stepped back.

"What?" Peterson demanded.

"Let's just say we're working a case about some missing plutonium and let it go at that."

"He's got a death wish," Peterson growled. "We just may have to oblige him."

"I'll do it." Dave stood up from the bumper. "My lunch was in the car he blew up."

"Oh, Brad," the mechanical voice cut in. "Don't get any wild ideas about putting a bullet in me."

"You can count on it—"

"Any drop in my blood pressure monitor will trigger a transmitter to send the *DETONATE* code to set off the other nukes, and get a load of this. If you put a round in the blood pressure monitor, the results will be the same. Armageddon." He laughed like the crazy bastard he was. "Is that fucking great or what? You dumb fucks are screwed no matter what you do."

Brad's heart rate shot up a notch. "What do you want from us?"

"I'm going to take a little nap, and that'll give you boys time to figure out what the hell I want from you. Remember, I have four nukes left, and one is here on my property. While I'm sleeping, attack me only if you want to get your own asses vaporized along with a large portion of the city of Lakewood."

Peterson glanced at the housing developments to the north and east. Thousands would die, he was sure. He waved over a patrolman. "Start the evacuation of everyone within a five mile radius."

"Yes, sir."

The electronic voice came back. "Have a nice afternoon, Brad. I'll call you at 6pm sharp. Oh, I almost forgot. If you're thinking about taking me alive, you can forget it. You won't live long enough to get to my steel front door. The entire area is rigged with land mines. Remember, you're not dealing with a nineteen-year-old kid high on coke." Darth Vader hung up.

"Word just came in, sir," the porky agent said solemnly. "Arches National Monument was just hit by a nuclear blast. Dozens of tourists are feared dead."

Brad dropped the phone. "We are so screwed."

***

"I'LL LET THE COPS stew for a while." The killer removed his Darth Vader mask and turned on the TV: *Breaking News* on Channel Eight. Okay, he lied about never watching Channel Eight. And come to think of it, he lied about never lying. He sat to watch the news anchor cry openly in front of the entire world. "They're all dead," he sobbed out. "They were on *Copter Channel Eight*: Sara Sutton, our traffic reporter and daughter of Judge Henry Sutton, the pilot, Bob Landen, and Annie Young, an intern here in the news department." He took a moment to compose himself.

"The Lakewood Fire Department suspects a fire in the cockpit brought the helicopter down in an open field. No one on the ground was injured. Unsubstantiated rumors say the helicopter was hit by a missile. At this time we believe the rumors are false. The NTSB is investigating."

The killer stood and shook his finger at the TV. "Wrong. You bozos got it wrong. Misinformation and lies, as usual."

Text running across the bottom of the screen reported the news he had been waiting for: *A Methane Gas explosion has destroyed a two-mile radius of Arches National Park in Utah. It is not known whether there were any fatalities or injuries from the explosion.*

Now the killer was really pissed off. The FBI was sweeping the truth under the carpet. It was no goddamned methane explosion. What the fuck was the FBI doing, trying to prevent panic among the sheeple? One thing was for sure. Brad believed him now.

***

THE STANDOFF AT THE Alamo stretched through the afternoon. Relentlessly, *Anything Goes* played on the remaining three speakers, louder than ever. The FBI could do nothing until 6:00pm when the suspect was due to call back.

Brad Tillman leaned against the fender of his black SUV and sipped lukewarm coffee from a thermos lid, thinking about his next move. A quarter mile down Morrison Road, a Blackhawk helicopter landed in a fury of dust. He tossed the dregs of his coffee in the gutter and watched a fifty-something-year-old man jump out and sprint his direction.

When he arrived, he asked Brad, "Are you in charge?" somewhat winded.

"Who the hell are you?"

"Harold Bertrum, National Security Agency." He stole a breath. "I'm in charge now."

"Who says so?"

"The President." He squinted in the direction of the white fortress. "How can you stand that music?"

"Don't worry. It kinda grows on you."

Bertrum huffed. "Then that's the only good news. We've determined your suspect has exactly what he says he has...plutonium."

"You just figured that out?"

"A shipment was stolen from a delivery truck en route to the depository at the Lawrence Livermore Laboratories."

"Tell me something I don't already know."

"He doesn't have enough for five bombs. Two maybe three, max...unless he has fifty-thousand centrifuges to enrich the uranium he'd stolen. We won't know which bombs are real or fake."

"Great," Brad grumped. "Nuclear Russian roulette?"

"This guy is a domestic terrorist worse than Timothy McVeigh. Find out what he wants and why. Make no attempt to storm his house or to harm him. We have to keep this thing under wraps. If word gets out that a maniac has nukes and no qualms about using them, panic would spread all over the country. Silence is paramount. Got it?"

A pissed-off Brad Tillman replied, "What do you want me to do, kiss his ass?"

"I want you to find out everything you can about him."

"We don't even know his name."

"I know something about him already. He has to be a nuclear physicist with one hell of a workshop. As we speak, our people are scouring records for dissidents or begrudged workers. What do you know about his personality?"

"For that, you need to talk to the Lakewood cop who's had more dealings with this guy than anyone else." Staring at Bertrum, Brad shouted, "Hey, Dave, the all-mighty NSA wants your help."

Dave field stripped a cigarette he'd just lit. Judging from the debris around the SWAT truck's back bumper, it appeared this experience had rattled his nerves to the max. As he walked over, he brushed mud from his still sopping uniform shirt then stared at Bertrum's concerned face. "Officer Dave Hinton. What can I do for you?"

"What do you know about our suspect?"

"Not much more than he's nuts to the moon."

"Did you get a look at him?"

"I only saw him for a moment, scrawny guy wearing a Darth Vader mask. I think he's just acting like he's crazy, but rest assured, he's crazy like a fox. For some reason he's pissed off at the world."

Bertrum arched a brow. "Revenge?"

"I don't know. He told me that he hoped the FBI would bring a forensic psychiatrist with them."

"I don't know about a forensic psychiatrist," Brad put in. "But our hostage negotiator just arrived. She's the redhead over by the black Crown Vic with all the cops standing around her. When the suspect calls back at 6pm, I hope he'll talk to her."

"If he doesn't call," Dave said, "we've traced his number. We'll call him if we have to."

"Got a name with that number?"

"Rumpelstiltskin."

"Fuckin' lot a good that does us." Bertrum glanced around. "I wonder what he's doing right now."

"He said he was going to take a nap."

Dave was right.

***

LYING BACK IN HIS recliner by the balcony, the man the cops would love to apprehend did what he had done every time he slept during the last five years. He dreamed the same dream. The dream always started the same way: his wife, Alice, sauntered over to the Lazy Boy recliner he was reclined in, pulled the newspaper off his face, and woke him up. "Jerry...Jerry..."

"Huh?"

"Jerry, I'm going to go pick up Brenda at school, and then we're going shopping for her cheerleader outfit. Do you want to go with us?"

"No. I'll stay here." He pulled the paper back over his face.

Jerry regretted that decision every minute of every hour of every day since then. He dreamed of that terrible moment when he answered the door later that day.

Two faceless Lakewood Police officers stood on his porch. "There's been an accident," one of them said.

"An accident?"

"Your wife and daughter have been killed."

Shock, like a baseball bat to his forehead, numbed him. "There must be some mistake."

"They were hit head-on by a drunk driver," the other officer said. "He suffered only minor injuries."

"No, not my wife and daughter. The Lord Jesus would never allow such a thing to happen to them."

"You can come down to identify the bodies if you want."

"There's been some mistake." He fell to his knees. "Some mistake, some mistake, some mistake..."

No sooner had he closed the door when there came another knock. Through tear-streaked eyes he saw Major Tom Jackson of the U.S. Army standing solemnly before him. "Jerry Hanson..?" the Major asked in a military tone.

"Yes?"

"I'm sorry to inform you that your son, Staff Sergeant Jerald L. Hanson Jr. was killed in action outside the town of Marout, Afghanistan, by sniper fire on 22 April 2024. The United States of America is very sorry for your loss."

Jerry continued to dream though his subconscious scream should have awakened the dead.

Now he stood at the funerals for Alice and Brenda and then suddenly the funeral for his son. Religious zealots came to protest: a Reverend Dolbert and his nine daughters, calling Sergeant Jerald Hanson Jr. a fag fighting for the Sodomites. The ugly daughters held signs that read: *God punishes dead soldiers by making them burn in hell.*

"Go away, go away, go away." Jerry tossed in his sleep. The clock radio came on. He reached over his wife's sleeping body to turn it off, just like he'd done nearly every morning for all the years they were married, but this morning was the next morning after the funeral, and her side of the bed was empty and cold. He sobbed as the radio relentlessly played: *Anything Goes.*

He stood in the courthouse for the trial of the drunken asshole who had caused the wreck. Smiling faces, laughing faces from his family, blank stares from the galley as Judge Henry Sutton hammered his gavel: "Six months in jail, suspended. One year probation." The killer of Jerry's family was born the son of a rich and influential Senator from Wyoming. Alice and Brenda meant nothing to any of them.

He screamed and screamed and screamed...

The phone rang and mercifully interrupted Jerry's dream. He awoke with a start, knowing it wasn't a dream...it was reality in its worst form, relived time and time again. He shook off the terror, heard *Anything Goes* still playing on the loudspeakers, and the phone kept ringing. The display showed Officer Dave Hinton's mug. Jerry became enraged that the cops had traced his number, and he was not about to take any shit off them.

He quickly donned the Darth Vader mask and picked up the receiver. "I'll blow all you cocksuckin' sons of bitches to hell."

"You said you'd call us at 6:00."

Jerry inhaled a breath to put himself back into character. "Dave, buddy? Is that you?"

"It's 6:30, so that's why I called."

"How about that. You missed me."

"You win. Your bomb threat is real. Come on out. Let's talk."

"Being nice and sweetzie isn't going to make me walk out and give up, Davey boy."

"I didn't think it would."

"So, you got a body count of how many assholes I sent to hell in Utah?"

"Thirty-seven. A party of National Rifle Association members and a Mormon church group out of Salt Lake City."

Jerry felt a feeling of joy for what he had done. "The country will just have to muddle through without those brave NRA cocksuckers fighting to defend our Second Amendment rights. As for the Mormons, I did them a favor. Church people love to say how they can't wait to meet Jesus, so it looks like I arranged a get-together for them. They should thank me, uh, no they can't thank me. They're all dead." He laughed. "Maybe their last thoughts were *Praise the Lord and pass the ammunition.* Now what can I do for you, Dave?"

"You said you wanted the FBI to bring along a forensic psychiatrist. We have one here. Doctor Joyce Taylor. Would you like to talk to her?"

"Sure, Dave, put the fucking bitch on the phone."

"Now be nice to her." Dave handed the phone to Joyce.

"Hello, ah..." She fingered her crucifix necklace and measured her words very carefully. "You can call me Joyce. To whom am I speaking?"

"I'm the guy in the house, you dumb bitch."

"You're not afraid to tell me your name, are you?"

"I'm not afraid of nothing. You can call me Jerry."

"Is that your real name?"

"Maybe, maybe not, but it'll do for now. Besides, I know you're trying to trick me. The only reason you want to know my real name is so that you can gather information and use it against me."

"I'm not against you, Jerry. I'm on your side."

"Like hell. You'd love to see me locked up in a padded cell so you can study me and pump me full of your psychotropic drugs and shock my ass with electro therapy.

Isn't that right, honey?"

"The police want the information to throw you in prison. I'm more interested in what makes you kill without remorse. It's not my job to judge you."

"You only assume that I don't have any remorse or feelings of guilt. You don't know that for a fact. Maybe I'm just pissed off at the world or maybe I suffered a great loss of my own. Could be because the Broncos didn't make it to the Super Bowl last year."

She blinked. "What has your problem got to do with bringing so much sadness to people you don't know and who have done nothing to you?"

"Let me explain it to you this way, sweetie: As Calibos suffers, so will all of Argos. I promise you."

"I have no idea what that's supposed to mean."

"I didn't think you would. You've spent too much time studying how everyone else's brains work instead of enhancing your own brain."

Her lightly freckled forehead creased. "Jerry, you asked for a psychiatrist. You must have had a reason. What reason is that?"

"The reasons will become clear to you in the near

future. Meanwhile, Joyce, would you mind doing me a little favor?"

"What do you need, Jerry?"

"I see on one of my monitors a couple of cops in camouflaged uniforms creeping up on my fortress. I bet they think you have distracted me. Tell them to stand up and walk away while they still can. And Joyce, don't pull this shit on me again."

Joyce pointed at Lieutenant Peterson. "Call off your men right now and don't ever use me as a decoy again."

The two encroaching cops stood up, and holding their rifles over their heads, walked backwards toward the brick wall. One of them stepped on one of Jerry's antipersonnel land mines. The policeman heard the click from the trip switch and froze in his tracks. He slowly squatted down, being careful not to move his foot. If he lifted it, he would be dead. The young SWAT officer screamed, "You have to help me. Can these be set off by remote control if that guy wants to?"

Jerry walked out on the balcony with a phone in one hand and an apple in the other. "Joyce, put Brad back on."

"This is Brad."

"Looks like one of your boys got himself fucked in the ass real good."

"Look, Jerry, or whatever your real name is, are you going to get your rocks off by killing some poor guy for only following orders?"

"Tell you what, Brad. It was you who put those cops in harm's way, not me."

"Lieutenant Peterson ordered his men to go in. He's in charge of SWAT. It's his officers that are in trouble, but they're my brothers in blue."

"Okay. I can use some entertainment. I'm going to let the bomb squad boys work their way to him and try to disarm the mine. I suggest those boys take care or they'll get their butts blown away. Oh, I almost forgot, if I see anyone trying to defuse any other mines, all hell will be unleashed on them. Got that, Bradley boy?"

Resigned to defeat, Brad replied, "We'll follow your directions to the letter. Thank you."

"There, see? Finally, I get a thank you. I'm feeling mighty generous right now."

Brad handed the phone back to Joyce. "He's a lost cause."

"Jerry?" she said softly. "Can I take a break to use the ladies room? I'll call you back in a little while."

Jerry laughed and blurted out, "Go piss to your heart's delight, kid."

Joyce set the phone down. "He's not insane."

Peterson huffed. "He sounds insane to me."

"Something made him snap."

Dave, leaning up against a police car with his arms folded, looked at Joyce. "Crazy is as crazy does."

Brad asked, "What was all that shit about Calibos?"

A rookie cop spoke up. "It's a line from an old movie, *Clash of the Titans.* Thetis, a sea goddess who lives on Mount Olympus, begs Zeus to forgive her son Calibos for his sins. Zeus refuses and turns Calibos into a lonely monster all the people of Argos fear. So Thetis says to her sister goddesses, "As Calibos suffers, so will all of Argos." The moral of the story is that Thetis lost the only one she ever loved so she wanted everyone to lose someone they loved so that they would suffer like she did."

Bertrum said, "That means our suspect lost someone he loved so he wants to make everyone else suffer...like he's suffering."

"He needs to be institutionalized," Joyce put in. "He's not a criminal. He's sick."

"Revenge may be a motive for his madness, but he's not acting in a moment of passion. This is premeditated, which makes him a criminal in my book. Anybody have any ideas on how we can get this guy alive?"

The rookie cop, Ronald Peoples, rubbed his chin, then: "There might be a way. We know he has the place totally surrounded with land mines. It's safe to assume that he doesn't have any such explosives on the roof. We bring in an ex-paratrooper, someone like me, drop him from a plane, and let him land on the roof. Once he's down, he lowers himself to the balcony and takes the suspect into custody."

Brad had to laugh. "Just like that? What do you think Jerry will be doing while all this is going on, playing Solitaire?"

Officer Peoples replied, "Sleeping."

Now Bertrum laughed. "How are we to know that for sure, kid? It's a suicide mission."

"We hire a plumber to scope out the sewer line with one of those cameras on a flexible cable to locate the vents, and instead of using a rotary pipe cleaner to clear out roots, wrap it with rags and use them to plug the vent pipes. Then we wire-tie a long hose to the camera cable and pump in an odorless sleeping gas, like they use in operating rooms, thought the toilet water. With *Anything Goes* blasting from his speakers, he won't hear any sounds made in the pipes. Before the suspect realizes he's sleepy, he'll be out like a light."

A very excited Bertrum spoke up. "Get on it right now."

***

J ERRY LEANED ON THE balcony railing and watched as the bomb squad slowly worked their way toward the cop standing on the land mine and his partner who was afraid to move.

What a bunch of dodo birds.

Jerry pulled up the Darth Vader mask and took a bite out of the apple. He saw SWAT team members and Lakewood police stationed in an arc within fifty yards of the perimeter wall. They had binoculars pointed right at him. Jerry promptly gave them the finger and went back to the apple and the cops' predicament. The bomb squad dildos were taking great care to get through the mine field. It took them the better part of two hours to rescue their stranded cops.

After watching them make it to safety, Jerry sat down to watch the local news and slowly drink a beer. He then had another. There was nothing on the news about him. The cops were doing an excellent job of keeping the situation under wraps.

I'll have to change that real soon.

He walked over to the sink and put a dirty plate into the dish water. Yawning, he moved to lie down in his recliner but decided to take a leak first. Damn, he was getting very sleepy. As he started to piss in the toilet, he noticed that the water in the bowl was bubbling. "What the hell?" He staggered over to a cabinet where he kept a gas mask. *I can't let myself pass out or all will be lost, all lost. The sons of bitches are pumping in Halothane gas.*

He put on the mask and plugged the toilet with a towel then turned on an exhaust fan. By this time he was seeing double and felt sick to his stomach. Waiting for his head to clear, he turned out the lights and sat in a rocker with an AR-15 rifle across his lap. Those bastard cops were up to something, but whatever it was, he'd be ready for them.

***

AN HOUR PASSED on a dark and moonless night.

Jerry thought about how ironic it was that he'd almost fallen victim to the same gas he'd used on Reverend Dolbert and his nine daughters. One night, during their all-night vigil of praying that the Lord would kill all the Sodomites in the country, he'd pumped the gas into their church. Then he rushed into the church and collected all the daughters and the reverend.

When they recovered from the effects of the gas, they found themselves tied up in chairs in an old dank building. They sat there wiggling and doing their best to break free of the ropes that held them, but to no avail. In the darkness they whispered to each other then they heard the clank of an iron door followed by a blast of flames that illuminated the room. The door clanked again and the firelight vanished. At first, they thought they were in the basement of an apartment building with a coal-fired furnace, but when the lights finally came on, they saw sheet-covered bodies on steel gurneys and realized they were in a mortuary...a crematorium to be more precise.

One of the daughters gasped and screamed in fear. At that moment, Jerry walked up behind them. He swung a dead cat by its tail, and without saying a word, he walked over to the furnace, opened the iron door, and threw in the dead cat. The body was engulfed in flames and began to make popping noises as it burned.

He remembered how the fire illuminated the horror on their faces, and how each one of them looked terrified when he told them that, soon, each of them in turn would be joining the cat. They all began to scream at him at once, so he gagged all of them except the Reverend Dolbert.

The Reverend, who had managed to piss all over himself, begged for mercy. "Why are you doing this terrible thing? Please let my daughters go, please, please." Then the reverend began to sob.

Jerry announced to the condemned that they had met him before at his son's funeral. "Remember how you taunted me? You carried signs that disrespected my son's sacrifice to this country, my sweet and noble son, and how God punished him by making him burn in hell. And one of you cocksuckers smeared dog shit on my car."

"We have our First Amendment rights," the reverend shouted.

"But you violated my rights in the process. Now I'm going to punish you for that. I've found you all guilty and sentenced you to death."

"Have mercy on my daughters."

"Do any of you really believe you'll receive pity from me?"

With that he dragged the reverend's chair over to the furnace door. When Jerry opened the iron door, the blast of heat curled the reverend's hair. He screamed. "No, please." Mercilessly, Jerry shoved the chair closer, but the reverend braced his feet against the furnace opening. "No. No." Jerry turned him and the chair around, and while suffering blows to his chins from the reverend's kicking feet, he shoved the preacher in head first and closed the door.

His daughters could hear their father's muffled screams.

Jerry stood before the girls. "Let's all bow our heads."

The preacher was still screaming. The heat should have seared his lungs and boiled his throat by now. Getting a little annoyed, he stormed to the furnace and opened the door. "Shut the fuck up. We're trying to say a prayer to Jesus to have mercy on your sorry, burning soul." He slammed the furnace door. All he heard now was the sobbing of his daughters.

After ten minutes he opened the door so that the daughters could behold his handiwork. Reaching in with a long bar he pulled out the charred and withered remains of the reverend. The whole place now smelled like burnt barbeque. "This is what hell is like, girls."

Jerry noticed that the oldest and plumpest daughter was already dead, probably of a heart attack. It was then that he decided to have pity on them. He walked up behind each chair, pointed his old army Colt .45 at the back of each of their heads, and pulled the trigger. By the time he was done, blood and brain matter lay splattered all over the floor.

At a quarter to midnight, just as he was reliving how the last daughter had died, he heard a prop plane fly overhead.

#

Officer Peoples checked all the straps to make sure they were tight around his chest and waist. He glanced at the pilot, gave him a thumbs-up, and then stepped out into space. He had a perfect view of the field and the lighted streets a half mile to the north and east of the Alamo. He pulled on the cords and put himself in a sweeping spiral descent. Each revolution brought him closer and closer to the house. He saw all the police cruisers turn off their lights, all except one, whose lights blinked twice to confirm the operation was a *GO*.

He glided down to the roof.

#

It hadn't dawned on Jerry what the cops were planning until he heard a thump on the roof. "Shit. The balcony." He sprang from the chair, stood in the center of the dark room, and pointed the rifle with the laser sight out the door at the balcony. His panicked breathing sounded shallow and labored inside the gas mask. In the dark, he saw a rope dangle down from the roof. Next he saw the silhouette of a man climb quietly down to the balcony floor.

Dumb bastards thought I'd be sleeping, huh?

#

Officer Peoples turned his back to the house and, using a black light, announced to the police via a quick series of flashes that he had successfully landed. He turned around and faced the house, prepared to be the rookie who'd made the greatest arrest in history. Peering into the dark house, he saw a tiny red light beyond the doorway. He thought it was a light on some electronic device. Then he saw a red dot on his chest. The last words he muttered on earth were: "Oh, fuck!" He saw the flash from the rifle but never heard the report as the bullet tore through his heart. His body fell backward and over the balcony. He landed on the driveway with a thud, but only after his head hit the mirror on the Mercedes' passenger side, which knocked it loose and left it dangling on its wires. His time as a policeman had come to an end at age twenty-three.

#

Brad shouted, "What the hell was that gunshot? Who fired? Our guy or the guy in the house?"

A SWAT team officer reported, "Our officer is down. I can't see him now from my vantage point. The shot came from inside the house. I saw the flash in my infrared binoculars, but it blinded me for a couple seconds. When my vision cleared, the balcony was no longer occupied."

"Son of a bitch," Bertrum spat.

#

Jerry, in fit of rage, threw off the gas mask, but his next thought was to be sure the air was safe. After a mad dash to the bathroom, he yanked the towel out of the toilet. No bubbles. That was a good sign, but was the gas hose still in place?

He grabbed a crescent wrench from the drawer, unbolted the toilet, and moved it to the side. A flashlight revealed what lurked in the sewer pipe. "Will you look at that?" He was staring right at the camera cable. That's when he got a diabolical idea. He grabbed hold of the camera and started yanking the cable up through the sewer line.

#

On the other end of the line, the plumber watched in disbelief as his camera cable unwound from its spool at what seemed like a mile a minute. The monitor screen, which had been perpetually black, now showed a flurry of activity: a partial face, a ceiling, a floor, a doorway, a ceiling, boots running across carpet. "What the hell?"

#

Jerry pulled the cable out to the balcony and let the camera slip over the banister and down to where it pointed right at the dead cop's face. He was lying on his back with his head turned to one side. His eyes were wide open with a blank stare. Jerry dialed the cops and donned his Darth Vader mask.

"Are you getting this picture, boys?"

"We see it," Dave shouted. "Are you happy now?"

"No. I'm pissed, so you better listen up. I'm going to set off another bomb at 10:20am Eastern Standard Time."

"No, don't—"

"Shut up and listen. The time is a little clue for you. Also, if you assholes listen really careful to the words of *Anything Goes* you might figure out where the bomb is located. If you find it in time, call me and I'll be generous and send it the *shut down* code. Then you can take it apart. I'm sure you'll be impressed with my handiwork."

"We'll get your ass, motherfucker."

"Not a chance. You won't find any fingerprints. I'm not stupid. And you dummies won't learn my identity from my Mercedes' license plates or the house deed or even my phone number."

"Yeah, we know. Everything is in the name of Rumpelstiltskin."

"Clever, huh?"

"You made a mistake somewhere. We'll find it."

"Good luck with that."

"What about our man?" Dave asked solemnly. "Can we recover his body?"

"You can come over in the morning, say about nine and get your cop friend. What do you say about that, Dave?"

A long silence followed.

"Dave? What do you say?"

"All right. I'll say it. T-thank you."

"Look at that. A real man steps up to the plate. But you better not pump anymore gas in here or I'll put all of you cocksuckers to sleep, permanently vaporized."

"You wouldn't detonate the bomb here. You'd be killed too. Then what would be the point?"

"Did you hear me tell you I'm not stupid?"

"I heard you, just don't believe you."

"Well, believe this, Dave. A smart person builds a bomb shelter for his bomb."

"Fuck."

"One last thing, Dave."

"What?"

"Get some sleep. You'll need it."

Click.

#

Dave put the phone down and slumped on the couch in the living room of the house that belonged to the old man he had met that afternoon. They'd commandeered it for their temporary headquarters and command center. It seemed like a week ago this nightmare had started, instead of just a few hours ago. He looked at his cell phone and saw his wife had left him eight messages. He called her up. "Peggy."

"Where are you?"

"I've got some bad news."

"What's going on?"

"I won't be coming home anytime soon."

"The news on the TV said that some sort of hostage situation was in progress in Lakewood, has something to do with the helicopter crash. That's all they can report because you guys aren't releasing any more information."

Dave yawned. "I can't go into my problems, but hug the kids for me and don't forget to say your prayers when you go to bed."

"Is it that bad?"

"It is."

"I love you. Be safe."

Foreboding filled Dave's heart and spilled out with his voice. "I love you too." He hung up then looked at Brad who was reclined on the couch with his feet on the coffee table. "Is anyone working on the *Anything Goes* riddle?"

"The FBI, CIA, NSA, we're all trying to figure out where the bomb is planted."

Bertrum walked in with a fresh cup of coffee, and as if trying to exhibit his role as over-all in command, he stated matter-of-factly, "The NSA will locate the bomb."

Dave, tired and disgusted, fell back into the couch cushions. "When? After it goes off?"

Joyce, curled up in a lounge chair in the corner, didn't even open her eyes when she muttered, "He's not going to set it off. If we don't find it in time, he'll come up with a reason to extend the deadline. He wants us to find the bomb. It's part of some weird ego trip he's on."

Bertrum sipped coffee, then: "What if you're wrong?"

Joyce shifted upright in the cushy chair. "Then we'll have more dead people on our hands, so make sure you find it in time." She scrunched down and laid her head on the armrest. "What about officer Peoples? Who's going to contact his family?"

With a sheepish look on his face, Bertrum said softly, "That's up to the Lakewood Police Department."

Dave sighed. "We take care of our own."

Bertrum groaned. "I feel real bad for that young man. I'm sorry I approved the operation. This whole affair is getting me more than a little rattled."

Brad had to agree. "We all have our crosses to bear."

Joyce held the crucifix on her necklace and closed her eyes. "God help us all."

***

AT THE FBI's HEADQUARTERS in Quantico, Virginia, agents were studying the words to *Anything Goes*. At 5:35am Eastern Standard Time they thought they'd come up with a possible location and called Brad.

The chief investigating agent said, "The most obvious place the bomb could be is in the first few lines of the song. The lines about Plymouth Rock—"

"I know the song," Brad cut him off. "I've been hearing

it constantly for thirteen hours now. Plymouth Rock? Is that what you've come up with...he buried the bomb at the site where the Pilgrims supposedly came ashore in 1620? It's too simple. And if I recall, the site has an iron railing around it and a granite colonnade over it, and you can look down on the rock from the sidewalk and see the date 1620 carved in the top of the stone. It's a popular tourist attraction. There's no way he could have planted a bomb there without the State Park Service noticing...not to mention hundreds of tourists watching."

"It fits both clues," the agent insisted. "Plymouth Rock is on Eastern Standard Time and it's the only definitive location in the song. That's all we've got so far. Though we're still studying lyrics for more possible clues, we've sent a team to Plymouth, Massachusetts, just in case. They'll be there in thirty minutes."

"Jesus Christ, you guys are a fucking joke. Who's ever in charge of that operation, I want to talk to him as soon as he gets there."

"I'll have him call you, sir."

Brad hung up, looked around the room, and asked Dave, "Where did Bertrum go?"

"Back bedroom to get some rest."

"Plymouth, Massachusetts, could be blown off the face of the earth in a few hours, and he's sleeping. I wonder who's the most insane, the guy in the Alamo or us."

Suddenly there was silence.

Dave stood. "The music stopped."

While everyone in the room just remained motionless and stared at each other, Dave rushed to the window. It was pitch black out there. The only sound in the room came from a grandfather clock: *Tick, tock, tick, tock* then it chimed four times.

Joyce broke the silence. "He's trying to get under our skin, that's all. By turning off the music, he's letting us know he's still awake. Bet he can't sleep with all that noise, either."

***

AT 6:35am, BRAD'S PHONE rang. It was the FBI calling from Plymouth Rock.

Brad couldn't answer it fast enough. "What did you find?"

"This is agent Larry Miller—"

Before he could say anything else, Brad interrupted him. "Fuck the formalities, what did you find?"

"There's nothing here, Agent Tillman."

"What did I tell those stupid fuckers? No way could Jerry have planted a bomb in such a public place."

"The park service people keep it very clean. The only litter we found was a label from a can of cranberry sauce that was stuck on the rock."

"Well, shit."

"Sir, we've been all over every inch of the place with detectors, and everything within a five-hundred-yard perimeter. There's no bomb here."

Dave's phone rang. He looked at Brad. "It's Rumpelstiltskin."

"Hold on, Miller." Brad nodded to Dave. "Answer it."

He picked up the call. "Are you having fun fucking with us?"

"Hey, Dave..." Darth Vader's voice droned. "Are you glad I turned off the music?"

"Tickled."

"Got a good night's sleep, did ya?"

"I slept on the floor with a gun in my ribs. You tell me."

"Now, now, Davey boy. What do you say to your old pal?"

"We're not pals."

"Wow, did you get up on the wrong side of the floor."

"What do you want?"

"Two words, buddy, then we can get on with the business at hand."

"All right. Thank you for turning off the music."

"Gotta love that tune, huh. You miss it already, don't ya?"

"Like a root canal."

The loud speakers came to life again, blasting away with *Anything Goes*.

"Fuck." Dave's brain started to throb.

"Bet those G men are looking all over Plymouth Rock, aren't they?"

"Why are you wasting our time?"

"I'll tell you what, Dave-o. You know what I loved about Thanksgiving?"

"Turkey."

"It's *not* the fucking turkey, Dave, though my late wife cooked a great bird. No. The thing I liked best was the cranberry sauce."

Dave couldn't help but smile. "I like the sweet yams with those little marshmallows—"

"Focus, Dave. The Pilgrims never had any cranberry sauce. The Indians had cranberries twice the size of anything the Pilgrims had seen in Europe, but no fucking cranberry sauce."

"What's the point, Jerry?"

"Ask Brad if he likes cranberry sauce."

Dave rolled his eyes. "Brad, he wants to know if you like cranberry sauce."

"Cranberry..?" Brad got back on his phone with Larry Miller. "What about that cranberry sauce label?"

"Ocean Spray. It's a co-op."

"Any address on the label?"

"No."

"How about local cranberry growers?"

"Ah...there's one about a mile from here. It's wet harvest season. The cranberry bogs will be filled with about eighteen inches of water."

"Get your ass over there now. He may have planted the bomb in a cranberry vineyard. If it's under water now, it'll be a bitch to find."

***

AN HOUR LATER, Larry Miller and ten agents found themselves wading through water a foot and a half deep, pushing cranberries aside and peering to the mucky bottom. They had to be careful not to trip over the low cranberry vines.

An agent with a Geiger counter held the detector over the water and swept it back and forth. The meter started jumping and ticking. "It's in here somewhere...this way, I think." The men followed his lead. One tripped and went under. "Maybe it's this way."

The time was now 10:05 Eastern Standard Time. They were almost out of time. He called Brad. Brad told Joyce to call Jerry.

"The water is radioactive," she said, "but we can't pinpoint the bomb's exact location in the bog. Are our men in danger of radiation poisoning?"

"They'll be fine, though I wouldn't recommend canning the cranberries. The sauce might glow in the dark."

"So the grower's season is ruined?"

"Boohoo. Tell them to drain the bog. Then your boys can safely locate and remove my bomb. I've already sent it the *shut down* code, but it's still a live bomb and will have to be disarmed, but tell them not to fuck with it until I say it's okay. It might go boom."

"Thank you."

"For what?"

"For not letting the bomb go off. I knew you wouldn't. You're not a bad person."

"You don't know anything about me, bitch." He hung up.

***

PROMPTLY AT 9:00am, DAVE and two officers wheeling a gurney walked up the driveway, maneuvered around one of the mangled iron gates, and stopped as instructed. Dave made the call. "Is it okay for us to get our guy?"

"Sure, Dave," the irritating metallic voice said. "Come and get him, but just remember I'll be watching your every move. One step off the driveway, you're dead."

"Thank you."

"See? That's not so hard. Good boy."

Dave felt like a trained dog.

As they walked up the driveway, he noticed the digital clock on the porch wasn't reading the time anymore. It was flashing *0:0:10,* counting down to zero, and then starting over again at ten seconds. Made no sense to him.

They came around the back of the Mercedes and saw Officer Peoples lying there. Flies were already buzzing around the encrusted bloody hole in his chest.

Dave looked up to see Darth Vader looking down at him. Neither said a word. The two officers parked the gurney next to Peoples and carefully lifted his body onto the pad. Dave leaned in and rubbed his palm over the dead officer's face to close his glazed-over eyes. Then Dave looked back up at the balcony. "When is this going to end?"

The killer said in a determined tinny voice, "In a few more days. If you live through it, then you can go home."

"What about you?"

"I'll be dead, Dave."

***

BACK AT THE CRANBERRY bog, the FBI agents had located the bomb and removed it from the muck. They were looking at a steel box that was 18 inches by 24 inches by 19 inches deep with a clear top made of ¾-inch thick bulletproof glass. The bomb weighed a hundred ten pounds. It looked as if there was no way to open it. After cleaning off the glass, all they could see was a quartz crystal display that read: *Rumpelstiltskin in* glowing bright green letters. Everything else inside the box was covered by a metal plate. There was a small hole in the plate, and they noticed eight tiny mirrors located around the inside walls. The box was magnetized. As the bomb squad studied it, the display flashed a new message: *Bring me to Brad. You have three hours.*

The news was relayed to Brad.

"We can't fly it from Boston to Denver in three hours."

Dave was helping put Peoples' body into the Lakewood Coroner's van when Brad came running over. "Get that asshole on the line right now."

Dave dialed.

Anything Goes

Darth Vader answered the phone. "What's the matter? You forget something?"

Brad grabbed the phone from Dave. "This is Brad. The message on that bomb of yours is now telling us we have only three hours to bring it to Denver. Is that correct?"

"'Fraid so, Brad, but I'm going to help you out. There's a completely restored SR-71 Blackbird at Logan International Airport in Boston for an air show this weekend. It can make the trip in less than an hour."

"Are you nuts? How are we going to get the Blackbird?"

"Ask not, want not. You better get busy, chop, chop. And Brad, tell the pilots not to try to dump my bomb in the ocean. It has an internal compass, can't fly east with it for more than twenty-five seconds, otherwise you know what will happen. Boom! Lastly, don't try to blow it up. Let's say your explosive breaks the outside casing. Explosives expand at about 2200 feet per second. Electricity travels at 186,000 miles per second. Which one do you think is going to win that race, el Brad-o? The juice from the dead-man switch will get to the detonator long before the concussion can destroy it. Oh, one other thing, don't try to take it apart or burn through the glass with a laser in hopes of disarming it. Tampering would be a real bad idea."

Brad sighed. "Looks like you've covered all the bases."

"Home run, dude." Jerry laughed maniacally. "When the bomb arrives, bring it to my front gate. You better get busy. Time's a wastin'. Tick. Tick. Tick."

***

WITH ONE HOUR AND twenty minutes left, the SR-71 Blackbird lifted off the runway at Logan and climbed to 38,000 feet where it rendezvoused with three air tankers to top off its six tanks with fuel for the two-thousand-mile flight. Fifteen minutes later, it broke away, soared to 85,000 feet, and headed west at a speed of 2000 miles per hour. A sonic boom announced its departure. They wouldn't have a minute to spare.

***

BERTRUM CALLED a meeting with Joyce, Dave, and Brad. He posed a series of questions. "What are we going to do to get this guy? Secondly, what does he want? Third, why does he want the bomb brought here? Speak up. We only have about an hour until the bomb arrives."

Joyce spoke first. "He won't be taken alive."

Dave agreed. "He told me he'd be dead when this is over."

"That's what he really wants," she confirmed.

"But why bring the bomb here?" Bertrum grumped.

"It's my professional opinion as a psychiatrist that he wants to show off his bomb-making skills. If his sole purpose was to kill people, he would've let it go off at Plymouth Rock."

Brad leaned forward. "Everything is a game to him."

"I have a suggestion," Joyce threw in. "Let me meet him face to face. He wouldn't fear me."

Brad frowned. "So how do you propose to do that?"

"I'll convince him to let me into his fortress."

"Bad idea," Brad shouted. "A very bad idea. What if he lets you in and then ties you up and rapes you? You can't just call 911, and we can't get in to help you."

"He's not a rapist."

Dave jumped in. "Oh, that's good news. He's a killer so

he'll just kill you instead."

"He's a lonely monster, like Calibos. He won't kill me."

Bertrum asked, "What do you expect to accomplish?"

"More than what we are doing now. If I can talk him into surrendering, we can save a lot of lives."

Brad scoffed. "Don't even try to do it, Joyce. He's too dangerous."

Bertrum said, "Call him up and see what he says."

While trying to suppress a feeling of trepidation, Joyce dialed Jerry's number. She listened as the phone rang three times. No one answered. The call went to voice mail:

"This is Jerry, the asshole. Leave a message."

Joyce closed the cell phone, almost relieved that he didn't answer. She went out to the front porch of the house. Pangs of hunger began to gnaw at her. She sat down on the porch swing and put a peppermint Lifesaver in her mouth. It would have to suffice as breakfast. The phone rang.

"You didn't leave a message, Joyce." Darth Vader's mechanical drawl gave her a shiver.

"How did you know it was me?"

"The boys would have left a message. Let me guess. You want to meet me in the flesh, right?"

"What makes you think that?"

"Maybe I'm a better psychiatrist than you."

Bertrum walked out on the porch, noticed Joyce on a call. "That him?"

She nodded. "Okay, will you meet with me?"

"Sure, Joycie. Like they say on that TV show, come on down."

"I'll be right there."

"Not so fast."

"What?"

"Walk up the driveway to the Mercedes and strip to your under clothes. Then I'll tell you what to do next."

She looked up at Bertrum. "He says he'll meet me."

"It's your neck."

"Okay, Jerry." She hung up, and as she began the long walk toward the Alamo, Bertrum called out to her from the porch.

"You can still change your mind."

Joyce didn't look back, just shook her head and continued on her way to what she hoped would not be her death.

Moments later, standing by the Mercedes, she kissed

her crucifix and stripped down to her panties and bra.

#

Seeing an officer with field binoculars aimed at Joyce sent Brad into a rage. He yanked the binoculars from the shocked officer and screamed, "You look at her again, I'll break your fucking jaw then write you up for bleeding on my fist, you fucking prick."

The officer stammered, "I, I was just trying to see—"

Brad shoved the binoculars into the officer's chest. "I know what you wanted to see. Now get your ass out of here. Go direct traffic or something."

#

Standing in her bra and panties and pumps, Joyce looked up to the balcony where Darth Vader looked down at her. She held her hands out to her side. "Satisfied?"

"Not yet. Now go to the door and walk into the room then just stand there."

The steel front door slid open.

She followed Jerry's instructions and stood motionless as the steel door closed behind her. Feeling trapped and alone, she scanned the room. It was void of normal furniture. In the center of the floor stood a large table with a coffin on it.

She heard Jerry's mechanical voice say, "Now turn completely around 360 degrees. I want to make sure you're not carrying a small hand gun. I'd feel really bad to have to put a bullet in that sweet body."

She examined the layout of the room as she followed his instructions: the closed steel door, no windows, an open doorway across the room, dimly lit.

"I believe you're not packing heat. Now go through that doorway to the elevator. The door is open. See the dress on the floor. Put it on. It belonged to my late wife. God rest her soul. Don't take your shoes on the elevator. Throw them toward the front door. You can get them when you leave."

Joyce felt a rush of dread as the door closed and the elevator made its way to the second floor. She was about to meet the man who had held the entire country hostage for almost two days now. The door opened and she stood waiting for further instructions.

"Welcome to my humble abode." The voice was smooth and not threatening. "I've been looking forward to this meeting for about six months now."

Six months? How's that possible?

Stepping out of the elevator, she saw Jerry for the first time, sitting in a Kennedy rocker, rocking and drinking a Coke. The Darth Vader mask rested on the end-table beside him.

Her eyes dilated as she stared at him. It was not out of fear though. She felt calm, as if she knew she was the one person this man would never harm.

"Have a seat on the couch. I think people in your line of work love couches. Is that right?"

"That's just an old stereotype."

Joyce studied the man in the rocking chair. *Can he really be a homicidal maniac? He must be in his late fifties. He looks like someone's grandfather with white hair, bifocals, and age spots on his forehead. He wasn't a very big man, maybe a hundred fifty pounds but muscular.*

"So, Joyce, what can I do for you? Wait. Don't answer. I want you to use my phone and let your cop buddies know you're okay. I always wanted my daughter to check in so her mother and I wouldn't worry. Call Brad. He cares for you. I can tell."

Taking the phone, she called Brad. "Everything is fine. Jerry told me to call."

"Is he holding a gun on you?"

Jerry yelled, "If you're asking if I'm making her say she's okay, the answer is no, Brad."

Joyce handed the phone back to Jerry. He hung up.

"What's the casket for?"

"Well, Joyce, it's not for you. It's my ticket to Valhalla. In Scandinavian mythology, it's a place reserved for warriors killed in battle. I'll be dining with the Norse god Odin in just a few days."

"I don't know about Norse gods."

"Sure you do, but you won't be my Valkyrie when I leave this world. You took a comparative religions class in college. You were just trying to play up to me. Getting on my good side, huh? And what will you be doing, Joyce? You'll be outlining a book about your harrowing experience with a diabolical maniac. Hell, I can see it all now. Your book will be a bestseller. People love blood and gore, especially in this shithole of a country."

"How did you know that I took a comparative religions class?"

"I know a lot about you and Brad and Dave. In fact, Joycie, I know things I shouldn't know. That's why

Americans are fucked. The information highway steamrolled everyone's rights to privacy. Though it's easy to find out just about anything about anyone, you'll play hell finding anything about me."

"You covered your tracks, we know."

"I've planned all of this for some time now. The bombs were a challenge. I thought the hardest part would be getting the plutonium. It wasn't. The Secure Transportation Association just isn't all that secure." He laughed. "You know the interesting thing is how heavy plutonium is. Once you have it, making a bomb is fairly easy. I thought that getting the lithium deuteride would be hard. It wasn't. In case you don't know what the hell that is, Joyce, let me tell you. First though, you must cross your heart and swear that you'll never, never tell the secret that I'm going to tell you. Do you swear?"

She was never good at keeping secrets, but if she could keep him talking and get comfortable with her, she might have a shot at convincing him to give up. "Okay. I swear."

"Not good enough. You didn't close your eyes and cross your heart. So, you have to do it again. Ready?"

"Yes." She closed her eyes and crossed her heart. "I

swear. How's that?"

"You forgot to say *and hope to die*."

"I don't hope to die, Jerry."

"Good enough. So here's how it works. Lithium deuteride cannot explode by itself. Nope, nope, nope. It needs a little help. This is where the standard atomic bomb comes into play. Set it off first in very close proximity to the lithium deuteride and you instantly have a temperature of about twenty million degrees, plenty enough heat to produce hydrogen isotopes from the lithium deuteride. The isotopes then fuse, creating a very big bang. A hydrogen bomb nuke. It will make your average suitcase nuke look like a fire cracker."

"You made a hydrogen bomb?"

"So, Joycie, make sure you're not around here when my little bomb goes off."

"You'll incinerate every living creature within a fifteen mile radius."

"Yes, just to prove a point. You see, I've gone one step further than those know-it-all assholes in think-tanks all over this country could ever imagine. I'm not some super genius...well, okay, I guess I am, but there are others in this world who can do the same thing I did. I want you to think about it this way. If building a hydrogen bomb were hard, every dumb-ass, shit-hole country in the world wouldn't have Washington pissing all over themselves with thoughts of us being nuked. Bad news, Joycie. It's easy to build a bomb. Our government knows it, and their nightmares are about to come true."

"Please, Jerry, don't do this."

Joyce studied Jerry's face as he rocked back and forth faster and faster. He had spoken with pride in his voice as he described how he manufactured his bombs, but now his words came out in a spew of hateful venom.

"Armageddon will be hardest on all those billionaire slave masters who have bullshitted their way to the top one-percent in this country. The blood of our soldiers is on their hands, those brave and noble young men who died for our country's corporate interests around the world. Exxon Mobil in Iraq. McDonald's and Starbucks in Kabul. Our boys come back from the battlefield and are paid off with the slogan: *We thank you for your service.* Well, sweetie, that ain't good enough anymore."

She coughed.

Anything Goes

"Would you like a Coke?" he asked.

"No thank you."

"Then I'll continue. The secret to making plutonium reach a critical mass is all in the way you crush it. Now the best way is to form the plutonium into a circular shape and put it into a metal ball about the size of a tennis ball. Next, you put C-4 charges spaced at the right intervals around the ball. Set them off at the same time and you have an implosion and a critical mass. You can figure out what happens next."

Visions of mushroom clouds sprouting across the land made her throat go dry. "I'll take that Coke now."

Jerry pointed at the refrigerator, and Joyce went over and got a Coke. She saw a picture of a woman, child, and soldier on the counter, so she asked Jerry, "Who are they?"

"My wife Alice, daughter Brenda, and son, Jerald...they were my family, but they're with God now."

"I'm sorry."

"Don't be sorry for them or for me. Be sorry for your country."

"They look like such nice people. Would they approve of what you're planning?"

Jerry stood and walked over to the balcony and, after surveying the area and deciding that all was secure, turned and raised his index finger on his right hand to make a point. "They would think what I'm doing is unthinkably terrible. However, they know how I think and they would understand why I did what I did and what I'm still going to do."

"You sound like you believe in God, Jerry. Do you?"

"Yeah, but not the one you believe in."

"How do you know what I believe?"

Jerry stormed up to her, and Joyce backed up out of fear. He reached out and pulled the gold necklace from her neck, breaking the gold chain. "This goddamned cross you wear tells me what you believe."

"Jerry..." She reached out to touch him, but he flinched back. "I came here to ask you to reconsider your plans, to show mercy on this country you hate so much. Most of us are good people with good hearts—"

"That's where you're wrong, Joycie. This is Sodom and Gomorrah all over again. I shall smite thee as your God smote them." He pinched the crucifix between his fingers and held it out to her. "It's time for you to go. Here, take your cross and Jesus with you."

Her necklace was ruined and everything it stood for tarnished. "Please, Jerry. There's been enough killing."

"I think you're a real nice person, Joyce. The milk of human kindness seeps from your pores. I, on the other hand, have only blood coming out of my pores. It's a byproduct of working with plutonium, as you know. That shit is pretty nasty stuff. But I'm afraid the killing has just begun. Give Dave and Brad my regards."

Joyce just stood there looking at Jerry. A feeling of despair surged through her body. She had failed to break through the crust of the madman and reveal his inner goodness. Feeling helpless, she could only say, "Goodbye, Jerry. I'll leave the dress in the elevator."

"Wear it. My wife would want it that way. Maybe we'll meet again someday...if you have the misfortune to wind up in hell."

As Joyce walked down the driveway, she looked at the clock. Now it read: *0:28:16...15...14....* It was counting down like the clock at Cape Kennedy when NASA was about to launch a rocket.

The loud music started up again:

Anything Goes...

She knew Jerry was slipping deeper and deeper into insanity and no one could help him or stop him.

What will happen when the bomb arrives from Plymouth Rock?

***

WITH A LITTLE OVER five minutes left on the countdown clock, the bomb arrived at Jerry's front gate. He laughed and donned the Darth Vader mask.

Dave's phone rang again. "Now what?"

Darth Vader's voice said, "It looks like you fuckers made it in the nick of time. Now for the good news, Dave, tell Brad my bomb wouldn't have gone off anyway. I was just having some fun with you boys."

"Fun? Do you know how much it costs to fly a Blackbird: the special fuel, the in-flight refueling tankers, their flight crews, ground support, and two pilots? That refurbished air-show Blackbird hadn't broken the sound barrier since its last operational flight in October of 1999. Those pilots risked their lives so you could have a little fun?

That's some crazy shit, man."

"Relax, Dave. Now the real fun begins. I want to see how brilliant those boys in the bomb squad really are. Put up a tent on the lawn and put the bomb on a very sturdy table under the tent. I wouldn't want any of you boys to get sunburned."

"This is bullshit. I bet this bomb is a fake."

"Be careful, Dave. The bomb is real. You've seen my countdown clock, right?"

It had been reset: *44:58:47...46...45...*

"Is that how much time before another bomb goes off?"

"That's how much time until this all comes to an end and everybody goes home happy."

"Everybody? What about you, Jerry? Will you be happy?"

"I'll have the satisfaction of getting my pound of flesh. Think of it as the *Eloquence of Revenge*. Is that fucking great or what?"

After hanging up the phone, Jerry took off Darth Vader and watched intently as the bomb squad picked up the hundred-ten-pound nuclear bomb and set it on a sturdy oak table that they'd taken from the home of their temporary headquarters. None of the team members wore their customary bomb blast protection suits, helmets, or gloves. If the bomb went off in their faces, no amount of armor would save them. Now they waited for the tent to arrive as per his instructions. Meanwhile, he watched them set up a series of lights around the bomb so that they could work into the night if they had to.

"Fools." He chuckled.

***

BERTRUM HAD INSTRUCTED the NSA to track all the cellular signals emitted from his fortress. Sitting on the same porch swing Joyce had been sitting on earlier, he had a look of satisfaction on his face, as if he'd just won a great victory.

Joyce strode over with Brad, and she sat next to him. "Why so smug?"

"We're going to get him now," Bertrum exclaimed.

Brad leaned on the porch rail. "How?"

"His computer is set to constantly relay code signals to the various locations where his other nukes are located.

Using triangulation, we're narrowing down the locations, block by block. We'll find all his bombs. He was a fool to let us examine his bomb from Plymouth, Massachusetts. From it we were able to trace the IP address, and pretty soon we'll hack into his Wi-Fi."

Joyce shook her head. "He's not stupid, believe me. He's betting that's exactly what you'll do. I just spent the better part of an hour talking to him, and I'm sure he's playing you all for the fools. Do you really believe he didn't know you would track the cell signals coming from his computer?"

Brad agreed. "He's always been one step ahead of us."

Bertrum folded his arms across his belly. "Sounds like you guys are on his side."

Joyce glared at Bertrum. "Go to hell." She got up and stormed into the house.

"I think you bonded with him," Bertrum yelled. "Hostages have been known to do that. The Stockholm Syndrome...I'm sure you've heard of it. Or maybe there's some hanky-panky going on between you two."

Joyce opened the screen door and shouted, "Do I look like a hostage, you jerk?"

Brad stood upright and glared at Bertrum. "And she's not the hanky-panky type."

Bertrum huffed. "Just wait and see. We'll have all his fucking bombs and he'll be in handcuffs by nightfall."

***

JERRY WATCHED WITH GREAT interest as the bomb squad carefully examined his nuke device. They were taking pictures and scanning it with meters. One guy even had the nerve to tap it with a hammer. Jerry, as Darth Vader again, called Dave. "You guys look like a bunch of monkeys fucking a football."

"What do you want?"

"I have something I need to work on but I'll be watching all of you. Don't contact me for thirty-two hours."

"Thirty-two hours? Are you fuckin' kidding me? What if we dismantle the bomb before that? Then what?"

"Don't worry, Dave, you won't." He hung up and laughed.

***

Anything Goes

AS THE BOMB SQUAD pondered their challenge, Brad folded his arms and watched with dread. He heard what sounded like a garage door closing and looked up to see steel panels dropping from the eves to the balcony, effectively sealing off the entire second story of the house. He wondered why Jerry was being so secretive about what he was doing. He looked at his watch. The time was now 4:44pm. He was about to order Chinese take-out for the bomb crew when an officer walked up with eight large pizzas. "These are compliments of the guy in the house."

Brad set the boxes on the table next to the bomb, selected a slice of cheese pizza, and took a bite. While chewing, he waved a gesture of thanks at one of the many cameras that were pointed at him.

#

Jerry didn't see Brad's gesture; he was on his way to his escape tunnel that led to an old brick-lined sewer dug in the late 1890s to direct street runoff from a Lakewood subdivision into Bear Creek. The project was abandoned in 1905 when a new drainage and sewer system was installed.

Practically no one even knew the old sewer ever existed.

Before it became a lifeline to and from his fortress, he'd thought of it as the *Bat Cave.*

Jerry slid down a fireman's pole he had built in the broom closet. It led to the sub basement. He walked past a coffin-sized chest freezer, its compressor humming, and one of his nukes, the display flashing STANDBY. Through a hole in the cement, he took the makeshift steps down to the ancient sewer.

He lit a flashlight he stored there and followed the tunnel almost three-quarters of a mile from his fortress to an old gated culvert on the banks of Bear Creek. He unlocked the bars with a key he'd stashed under a rock, and once out in the evening air, he re-secured the gate and walked across the road to the house where he once lived with his family.

The single-story house was exactly as it was the day he got the terrible news about his family. Dust lay on everything inside, giving the place a dull gray hue. His face was somber and his lips pushed tightly together as he walked through the living room on his way straight to his bedroom. Pulling open a dresser drawer, he took out his .44 Magnum and a hunting knife. As he left the room, he looked back at the unmade bed he and Alice had shared all those many years. An overwhelming wave of grief made him stop in the doorway where he stood bent over and waited for his head to clear. Grief had a way of punishing a man for loving a woman so deeply.

Determined to press on, he made his way through the kitchen to the garage. He didn't look back, as if he were afraid he might see Alice's ghost begging him not to kill again. He climbed into what had been his pride and joy in years gone by: a completely restored 1996 Chevrolet Corvette. He revved up the engine and remembered how the sound would make his daughter cover her ears and back away, laughing. At that time she only had less than ten years of life left to live. These thoughts made him more determined than ever to kill every fucker responsible for her death.

Stopping only for gas, he made it to Casper, Wyoming, in six hours.

***

AT 11:25pm, AT A HOLIDAY Inn in Casper,

Wyoming, a man in his early sixties and the keynote speaker for a dinner being put on for his favorite charity entered the restroom to use the toilet. As he headed for one of the stalls, he glanced at a man washing his hands. The man recognized him as the Senator from Wyoming. "Nice evening tonight, Senator Gee. The party is going well." He flicked water from his hands.

The Senator found all the stalls were empty and picked the closest one. "I'm looking forward to giving my speech."

"Good luck with that, sir."

The Senator started to close the stall door when it suddenly flew back into him and slammed him against the toilet. Fear instantly struck him in the chest. The man who'd been washing his hands now staggered about and held his hands up to his throat. Blood was pumping out a cut artery. A streak of blood on the stall door marked the spot where he'd been attacked. "What the hell?"

A white-haired, fifty-something-year-old man clutching a bloody knife stood right behind the mortally injured man, who suddenly slipped on his own blood and fell on the floor where he made choking, gurgling sounds.

The Senator was at a loss for words and in a state of

shock. For a few seconds he stood mesmerized as he watched the man bleed out. Then the Senator feared for his own life. "Please, mister, I didn't do anything."

The killer stared at him while he wiped the blood off the knife on his shirt. "Do you remember me?"

"No, sorry."

"Your son got drunk and killed my family."

Fear deepened the creases in the Senator's terrified expression. "Jerry Hanson?"

"You got him off scot-free." Jerry pulled the gun from his coat pocket.

"Please, no."

The Senator would not be the keynote speaker, after all. Two bullets from the .44 Magnum, equipped with a silencer, tore into his chest. He flopped back and fell to a sitting position on the toilet.

Then Jerry administered the coup de grâce. He put the barrel of the gun in the Senator's mouth and pulled the trigger. The bullet blew off the back of his head and penetrated a water pipe in the wall. As water sprayed on the Senator's open braincase, he fell off the toilet, which triggered it to flush automatically.

\#

Jerry, the killer of two men, stood there in the stall and watched the blood on the toilet seat drip into the bowl, turning the water crimson. Then looking down at the man with the slit throat, he said coldly, "Sorry, my friend. You're collateral damage. Nothin' personal." He washed his hands then calmly walked out of the men's room and made his way to the hotel's parking lot. His plan was working to perfection. Soon the whole country would mourn Senator John Nathan Gee's death, and anybody who ever was anybody important would attend the funeral.

He fired up the Corvette's engine and savored the roar. As his iPod played *Anything Goes*, excitement coursed through his body. It would only be just a little while longer before he'd find his Valhalla and be with Alice and Brenda and Jerald. He took his mind off his goal and began to gloat. It was then that he almost made a mistake. Using a burner cell phone, he dialed Brad's number to brag about his recent achievement, but realizing the blunder, he hung up before Brad could answer.

***

Anything Goes

BRAD, AT THE TIME, was eating dinner with Joyce at a Denny's restaurant. They sat across from each other in a booth, but he wanted to be closer to her. "Are you from around here?"

"Born and raised in Colorado Springs. You?"

"South Denver. There were six of us kids."

"I was an only child."

"Spoiled?"

"Sometimes."

Brad's cell phone chirped once. He looked at the display. *Call ended.* "Must've been a wrong number," he commented. "This is a secure line only used by the FBI."

"Jerry calls you on it."

"Okay, FBI business."

Joyce stopped eating her dinner salad. "Do you get many wrong numbers?"

"First one, actually?" Brad wasn't worried about the phone call. He was thinking about how gorgeous Joyce looked tonight and wondered if he had a shot with her. Still, he kept his demeanor professional. "So you think Jerry snapped due to a tragedy that happened years ago, and now he's a psychopath?"

Joyce sucked on a straw to get the last drops of Coke from her glass. "That's my professional opinion."

"You know the saying: the only good psychopath is a dead psychopath."

She leaned forward, her face a steely mask of serious resolve. "I want you to take him alive, Brad."

"And I want to sleep with you, Joyce, but we don't always get what we want."

She stared at him like he'd grown a second nose, then she smiled. "I'll make you a deal. Take Jerry alive and I *will* sleep with you."

Brad didn't have to try hard to appear shocked. "I can't believe you just said that."

"Hey, if he's alive, I get to study Jerry's mental derangement, and you get laid. We both win. Do we have a bargain?"

"Absolutely. But I'll have to get to him before Bertrum and the NSA. What do you think Jerry's going to do next?"

She set down her fork. "Okay. The bomb didn't go off the first time, and it's not going to go off this time. It's a diversion to keep you all busy while someone else dies."

"Who? One of our guys at his place?"

"No. He could've killed all of you by now. His next victim is somewhere else."

"But how, Joyce? He can't go anywhere."

"I wouldn't put anything past him. His favorite song is *Anything Goes*. You might want to check where that wrong number came from."

***

JERRY PARKED THE Corvette outside the cemetery where his family was interred. It was closed for the night. He shoved the gun under his belt behind him and climbed over the fence. As he walked across the grass, still wet from the sprinkler system that had just shut down for the night, thoughts raced through his mind:

Six years ago, I could never have imagined that I'd be sneaking into a cemetery right now. If someone had asked me what six years in the future would bring, I'd have said: our daughter is in college and will graduate soon, and Alice and I will be taking a cruise with our church friends to Bermuda in the fall, and Jerald will be discharged from the service and married with children.

Whoever coined the phrase *life is a bitch* missed the mark. Life is a fucking, fucking goddamn son of a bitch filled with misery that religious assholes try to paint over with "God loves you" salvation shit, as if that would keep death away from their door.

Well, it won't. I'll see to that. Tonight there are a lot of happy families who'll soon be crying over their dead relatives.

Jerry trudged slowly toward the marble mausoleum that held the remains of the sole reason for his existence. He slipped inside and walked through the dim light to his beloveds' crypts. He put his fingertips on the engraved names of Alice and Brenda and felt the depth and chill of each letter. Leaning over, he let his forehead touch the cold marble and envisioned them sleeping inside, each dressed in their prettiest gowns. He then put his hand on the crypt just below the other two, the resting place of his son. The images and sounds of a happier life warmed his heart. He stayed in that position for several minutes, reliving the memories of his family before tragedy, circumstance, and human mistakes shattered his world.

"Hey. You can't be in here."

Jerry turned into a flashlight beam that shined directly in his face. "I miss my family. I don't mean any harm."

"Don't move." The night caretaker made a call on his cell phone.

"9-1-1. What is your emergency?" echoed through the tomb.

"Got a prowler here."

"A unit is on the way."

He hung up his cell phone. "Okay, fella. I need to see some identification."

"All right, take it easy." Jerry reached to his back pocket as if to get his billfold but pulled the .44 instead. "Nobody can know I was here."

The caretaker only had time to drop the flashlight before one round ripped through his heart. He dropped with a thud and never made another sound.

Jerry stood over old man's body and muttered, "Yep, life is a fucking bitch."

He made a hasty retreat.

After the fiasco at the mausoleum, and knowing the police would soon be there collecting evidence, Jerry raced to get back to his fortress.

#

Meanwhile, Brad and Joyce, now holding hands, left the restaurant and made their way to Brad's car. Always the gentleman, he opened the door for her. She sat in the passenger seat, pulled the seatbelt across her body, and locked it into position. He bent in and pushed his lips tightly against hers. She responded favorably until he slid his hand up her thigh. Breaking the kiss, she pushed him away. "You haven't taken Jerry alive yet."

"Oh, I will. Just wait and see."

#

Jerry parked his Corvette in the garage and hurried back through the tunnel, thinking about his nuke and wondering how the bomb squad was making out.

Once back at his control center, he went straight to his monitors to see how things were shaping up outside. He zoomed in on Brad and Joyce who had just arrived to check on the bomb squad boys' progress. Using pry bars, they were prying on the glass lid, still trying to open the case. Jerry decided to go to bed, content that no one would dare to disturb his sleep.

Anything Goes

***

AT NINE IN THE MORNING, he got up and opened the shutters over his balcony. After turning up *Anything Goes* on the loudspeakers and with Darth Vader in place, he walked out into Colorado sunshine. He yawned and stretched then leaned on the railing and looked down at the agents, still hard at work under the tent. "How are things going, boys?"

Bertrum glanced up at him. "How are we supposed to open the case?"

Jerry laughed. "Doesn't matter how. The bomb's not going to go off anyway."

"You said you didn't disarm it."

"I lied."

"But the countdown clock's still running."

"You dumb bastards don't know the difference between the radioactive signature of radium and that of plutonium. I used to think you government boys were fucking smart. Well, excuse me."

"You mean it's a dummy bomb?"

"I couldn't have said it better myself."

The bomb squad techs dropped their tools.

"We're outta here."

"Fuckin' shit."

Jerry laughed. "Now I know how D. B. Cooper got away with $200,000 when he hijacked that plane back in 1971. He was dealing with the likes of all of you dumb asses."

"It was just his lucky day."

"I don't need any luck. There's no doubt that I'll win."

"Is that what this is all about? Winning? You kill people just so you can win."

Another voice said, "Did it ever cross your mind that you really are crazy?"

"Who said that?" Jerry demanded.

"I did."

Jerry leaned over the balcony and saw Dave. "Well, well, well. So how are things going with you, Dave?"

He stepped up beside Bertrum. "Everything isn't about you, Jerry. We've got another murder to solve at the cemetery."

"The cemetery? That's a horrible place to get murdered.

What is this fucking world coming to? Of course, on the bright side, I suppose there won't be any transportation charges involved in his funeral since he's all ready there."

"Hardy, har, har."

"Tell Joyce to join me for lunch, will you, Dave? And Bertrum, it's no big deal your bomb boys couldn't take my bomb apart. It wouldn't have done them any good to see how it works."

"I'll give them a break for now. They'll be back. We're going to crack this thing even if it kills us."

"I made each bomb different, and though all my anti-tampering safeguards may look the same, they don't work the same. In other words, fuck with any of my nukes, if you should find them, and somebody's city is going to be blown to hell."

"You're bluffing," Dave shouted up.

"All my other nukes are the real McCoy. Remember Utah? This one I built so I could have some fun with all of you boys. When I think about it, goddamn, I'm smart...or could it be everyone else is just fucking stupid?"

Brad rushed up the driveway. "Who's stupid?"

"Well, good morning, Brad. I'll cut you and Joyce a little

slack. Both of you show signs of intelligence. Bertrum, on the other hand, was not named head of the NSA, the National Stupid Agency, for nothing. I won't comment on Dave. He's just a dumb cop."

***

BACK AT THE HEADQUARTERS house, Brad motioned for Bertrum to come over to him. "We traced a signal from Jerry's computer to a farmhouse in Ohio. I guess you were right. He's just made his first blunder."

In a skeptical tone Bertrum said, "Farmhouse, huh?"

"Yup. A farmhouse, 221 Mockingbird Lane, five miles outside Columbus."

Bertrum dropped his coffee cup. "Is this a fucking joke? That's my house."

Brad, doing his best to stifle a laugh, said, "I guess we have to arrest you."

"It's a bogus signal, and you know it. There's no bomb at my house. He's fucking with you." Bertrum, red-faced with bulging veins in his neck, walked in circles and stomped his shoes on the floor. "I'm going to kill him myself."

"Okay. So you're going to kill him, but first we have to catch him, and time is running out on two fronts. The news hounds are getting persistent, and we still don't have a clue where those other nukes are located."

"Shit. This is a goddamned circus. He's making fools of us all."

Brad huffed. "Speak for yourself."

***

JOYCE HAD GONE HOME to her townhouse and was still asleep after the long night with Brad when she got a call from Dave.

"Jerry wants you to come over for lunch in two hours."

Joyce dutifully agreed and got up and went into her kitchen and turned on the TV while she made a pot of coffee. She watched with great interest the news story about the cemetery murder, sat down, and drank a glass of orange juice while the coffee percolated. She wondered about the killing. She started to take another drink of juice but stopped with the glass just inches from her lips when a thought crossed her mind. *Could Jerry's family be buried there?* "Son of a bitch."

She put down the glass and hurried to take a shower and put on her makeup; she couldn't get out the door fast enough. She drove straight to the cemetery and, wearing her jacket with its big and bold FBI yellow letters emblazoned on the back, walked past the Lakewood cops and into the mausoleum. Standing there with her arms folded, she slowly studied the blood spatter on the floor and the wall of crypts.

A Lakewood cop approached her. "Do you need anything?"

"No." Squatting, she lined up the blood trails with the column of crypts on the wall, figuring the fatal shot came from that direction. Slowly raising her eyes, she read the first crypt marker. *Doctor Burl Anderson - born: 21 January 1904 - died: 13 March 1965.* She looked at the marker above that one. *Janice Ann Carter - loving wife - born 20 May 1921 - died 22 June 1988.* It was the next marker that made a chill run through her body. It read: Sergeant Jerald L. Hanson Jr. - Our loving son - Born 14 April 2002 - Died 23 April 2024.

"Hanson," she muttered and continued upward. *Brenda Marie Hanson - born 26 November 2005 - died 25 April 2024.*

And directly above Brenda's crypt: *Alice Ann Hanson - born 22 January 1980 - died 25 April 2024.*

The names of Jerry's family members matched the names on the crypts. Jerry Hanson, distraught husband and father, had turned domestic terrorist. Shuddering, she took out her cell phone and called Brad.

He answered the phone. "Joyce? Where are you?"

Right as she started to tell him what she'd found, she decided on a different course of action. "I'm supposed to meet Jerry for lunch, but I'm going to be late. Maybe 4:00pm. Please relay this to Dave so he can tell Jerry."

"What are you up to?"

"Nothing...ah, just some work."

"Do you have anything to say to me after last night?"

She had to think fast. "I enjoyed our dinner date."

"And the kiss? What about that?"

She groaned. "The jury is still out, Brad."

"Thanks a lot. I'm not feeling real manly right now."

"I've got to run. See you this afternoon."

She drove to the Public Health and Vital Records Department for Jefferson County. It was housed in a glass-domed building made of precast crushed rock, set against the foothills, and referred to as the Taj Mahal. She knew that vital records were not in the public domain but could be reviewed by anyone who had a direct and tangible interest in protecting the deceased's personal rights, thus she figured she wouldn't need a warrant just to find out what had happened to Jerry Hanson's family.

Chin held high, she marched up to the clerk behind the counter. "I hope you can help me. I want to see the death certificates for Alice Ann Hanson and Jerry L. Hanson."

The clerk gave her two forms to fill out. "One for each name, please."

She filled in the *names* and *dates of death* from the inscriptions on the crypts. However, in the *place of death* boxes, she had to write *unknown*. Under *Reason for request* she wrote: *Official FBI murder investigation.*

Finished, she handed the forms to the clerk.

"That'll be twenty dollars each."

Joyce flashed her FBI badge. "I don't want copies. I just need to know how these people died. It's imperative to my investigation."

"In that case, just a minute, please." She soon came back with a couple file folders stuffed with papers. "I thought you might like to see everything we've got, but you can't take these papers out of here."

"Thank you. I need a private place...ah...your office will do, if you don't mind."

"Of course." The clerk let Joyce come around the counter and then led her to the office.

She sat down at the desk and began to look through the records. Alice Ann Pierson had married Jerry Leroy Hanson on June 17, 2000. There were two live births, Brenda and Jerald Jr. Alice's death certificate listed blunt force trauma, car accident. Brenda's death certificate was there too, same cause of death. Jerald had died in combat. She was studying the documents when two hands reached around her from behind and grabbed her wrists.

Panic belted her but quickly subsided when she saw those hands belonged to Brad. "How did you find me?"

"I had your cell phone tracked and put two and two together after the Lakewood Police called to find out why you were snooping around the cemetery crime scene. Now let me ask you..." He held her tighter. "What the hell do you think you're doing?"

"I'm doing your job. Besides, if I'm the one who takes

Jerry in alive, I'm off the hook with you."

"No way. If he lives, we're sleeping together, no matter how the collar comes down." He glanced around to make sure no one was watching then kissed her neck. "So what do you have?"

"Our guy is Jerry Hanson. Either he was at the cemetery last night or he has an accomplice who murdered the caretaker and probably helped him build and distribute the nukes across the country."

Brad had to hold back a laugh. "How did you come to this conclusion, may I ask?"

"Unless he can be in two places at once, he never left the Alamo last night."

"Are you sure about that? Like you said, he's been pretty resourceful throughout this entire caper."

"He'd have to dig a tunnel."

"Even for Jerry, that would be impossible."

"What about that wrong number? Find anything?"

"Burner phone. Dead end."

"We should head back. It's almost four o'clock. I don't want to be late for my lunch appointment with Jerry." She left the office and handed the folders back to the clerk.

"You've been a great help."

"My pleasure. Anything for the FBI."

In the parking lot, Brad walked her to her car. "So you think he's out for revenge for the loss of his family?"

"Justice failed him, and the country failed him. He has a death wish at the end of this. He's got nothing left to lose."

"But an accomplice to murder a cemetery caretaker? I don't see a connection."

"Find one...or prove he has a secret way out of his fortress."

***

As *ANYTHING GOES* BLARED in the background, Jerry overcooked two TV dinners in his microwave. He saw Joyce walk up the driveway. She stopped at the Mercedes and began to take off her dress, just as she did the first time. "Keep the dress on," he yelled down to her.

"What if I have a gun hidden in my panties?"

"I'll trust you this time. Come on in. You know the routine."

The steel door opened.

She left her shoes at the front door, got off the elevator, and stood there wondering why she didn't see Jerry. She walked to the balcony and looked down on the bomb squad boys again attempting to open the bomb.

Jerry stalked up behind her and looked over the railing. "I told you boys it's not going to go off. I'll even prove it, so get out of the way. Excuse me, Joycie. I'm going to help these dummies out." After picking up a Thompson sub-machinegun, he pointed it over the railing.

Seeing the weapon, everyone under the tent took off running in all directions.

Joyce backed away. "Don't do it, Jerry."

"I'm not going to shoot anybody." Jerry pointed the Thompson at the bomb and opened up on it. The bomb and the table were quickly reduced to a pile of junk.

Joyce stood there with a shocked look of disbelief.

He held out the still smoking machinegun to Joyce. "There are a few rounds left in the magazine. Take it and kill me with it."

"I don't want to kill you."

"Then let's eat lunch. I hope you like it. I've been

slaving over a hot microwave for hours. It's meatloaf and mashed potatoes. I've already put the food on the table. Sit down and I'll pour the wine."

Jerry's phone rang. It was Brad. "Boyfriends can be such a pain in the ass." He answered the phone. "Don't get your feathers in a ruffle. I told you the bomb was harmless."

"Fuck the bomb. Joyce better be okay or I'll be over there in five minutes to blow your fucking brains out."

"Whoa. Not only are your feathers ruffled, I believe you're madder than a wet hen."

"Put her on the phone now, you fucking asshole."

"Houston, we have a problem." Jerry held the phone toward Joyce. "Brad is worried about your welfare. Must be true love."

She snatched the phone from his hand and yelled at Brad, "What the fuck? I'm fine. There's nothing wrong."

"Nothing's wrong? What the hell is the matter with you? You're having lunch with a homicidal maniac and you say there's nothing wrong. Everything is wrong with that. I promise you this. When you get out of there, assuming you get out alive, you're never meeting with that nut case ever again."

"You're not my father, Brad."

"If you even think about seeing him again I'll arrest you for aiding and abetting a murderer and lock you up. Got it?"

Jerry had heard Brad's rant. "Father, boyfriend, pain in the ass, hey, he's got everything a woman could want."

"Goodbye, Brad, and don't worry. I'll make good on our bet as long as you don't come unglued." She hung up.

"Well, you don't say." Jerry smiled like the Cheshire Cat. "You two have a bet about me? How intriguing."

She looked out over the balcony, saw the police cars off in the distance and imagined the binoculars and rifle scopes aimed at him. Getting Jerry out of here alive seemed impossible.

"Joyce? Do tell me the details of your bet." His voice was filled with mirth.

"Well...it's embarrassing."

"All the better."

She steeled herself for a hardy laugh from Jerry. "I want you taken alive. Brad wants to sleep with me. So if we take you alive, I'm going to sleep with him. If you die, nobody gets laid."

"I'm so impressed with you right now." He held the

dinette chair for her. "Too bad poor Brad is shit out of luck."

"You mean..?" She sat.

He scooted in her chair. "Nobody is taking me alive."

She examined the TV dinner before her: black-edged meatloaf, mashed potatoes and wrinkled gravy, not enough corn to feed a bird, and apple crumple, the only thing that looked edible. He'd accented the meal with a pretty glass of red wine. Now that was a plus. He really knew how to treat a lady.

Sitting across from her, he announced, "I'll be resetting my doomsday clock tomorrow. Tell Brad to leave me alone, and if he's a good boy, I'll tell you where the other nukes are located, right before the clock hits triple-zeros. All will be disarmed...but one."

"One?" She tipped her wine glass to him.

He bumped her rim with his glass. "Insurance."

"So we do what you want?"

"Yes."

"After your dead."

"The good news is that you and Brad will be alive and you'll have a great story to tell your kids someday."

"I hope you'll change your mind about dying."

"I hope you'll change your mind about sleeping with Brad."

"Touché." That deserved a big gulp of wine.

"When I'm dead, I'll be happier. The human race wallows in the mud and the blood and the filth with the pigs, Joyce. Since I've always known this, I never did fit in. I thought I did...when I worked as a nuclear physicist for Lawrence Livermore Laboratories, but after I got laid off, I felt like an outsider. A nobody. Except when it came to my family. They needed me no matter what. Now that they've been gone for these past five years, I just want to be with them again...forever this time. However, there'll be more people who die before I do. Casualties will number in the hundreds. There's nothing on this earth that can save them now, not Bertrum, not Brad, not Dave, not the entire U.S. Fifth Army, or not even you pleading for their lives. As Caesar said when he marched against Rome, *Let the die be cast.* In a few days you'll understand why I scorched the earth to get my revenge."

She poked her fork at the overcooked meatloaf, her brain just as fried under his vision of doom.

"Oh. Sorry about the meatloaf. I've never mastered

cooking in a microwave, though I'm also an electrical engineer and know exactly how and why they work. You probably figured that out from our last discussion on how to make a nuclear bomb. I'm not a nitwit."

She tried the apple crumple. It looked much better than it tasted. "So, Jerry, we wallow in the mud and the blood and never get better as human beings. How does killing so many people make you any better than the rest of us?"

"Our weapons of war get deadlier with each generation, but the human race stays the same. A 21st century asshole is no different than a 1st century Roman asshole. We just eat better, that is if you forget about the meatloaf. Americans have lost the idea of blood justice, but I'll be bringing it back in a spectacular way."

She shuddered at what that might mean. "I like to think, that if we're wallowing with the pigs, some of us try to reach out to God for help and guidance."

"God has shied away from us, Joyce. I see his abandonment in everything around me, the decaying inner cities, the homelessness, the crime. I have to ask myself why. Maybe he doesn't want to get any pig shit on his face."

She set down her fork. "I'm not hungry anymore."

"What do you want to do now, kid? I can't compete with Brad as a lover, so there'll be no fooling around. Besides, I'm too old and I've only loved one woman in my sorry life. I know. Let's go downstairs. I'll need your help when I'm gone."

They got up from the table, took the elevator down, and walked over to the empty casket. Jerry ran his hand along the smooth side. "When the clock reads triple-zeroes, Brad's boys can storm the place with guns blazing. I won't care anymore. I'll be lying dead in this casket."

"What do you want me to do?"

"I don't want the coroner to desecrate my body with an autopsy. Don't let anyone take my body out of the casket. If they do, the last of the nukes will go off."

"Insurance?"

He nodded. "So I get my final wish. I'll leave instructions as to where and how I'm to be buried. There's an internal compass in the casket, and once I activate it before I die, you'll have only two hours to place me in my mausoleum crypt. If you don't... Boom!"

Her heart lurched. "So the last activated bomb is around here somewhere?"

"Joyce, I like you and Brad, so don't be anywhere near the casket should Bertrum choose to not believe me. Okay?"

"I wish I knew what this is all about."

"Soon enough, Joyce. You should leave now, otherwise Brad will worry. Would you like a doggie bag for your meatloaf?"

"Sure, why not?"

"Stay here and I'll get it for you."

Joyce walked around the room with a heavy heart and a deep sense of sadness. What a waste of innocent lives, and there'd be more killings before this was over. She was powerless to explain it much less stop it. In all her years in forensic psychiatry, she'd never met such a likeable, diabolic, and deranged murderer. Jerry Hanson would be one for the text books.

He got out of the elevator and handed Joyce the brown doggie bag. "Well, here you go, kid. I guess it's time to say goodbye. How about giving an old man a hug?"

Joyce hugged Jerry and, with tears in her eyes, did not look back as she picked up her shoes and walked out the front door.

Jerry hurried up to the second floor balcony, and seeing

Brad waiting in the driveway, sporting an M-16 rifle, he waved and yelled down, "You tell Brad he better be good to you or old Jerry will come back and kick his ass."

As Joyce walked toward Brad, she could tell by the scowl on his face that he wasn't happy. Thinking about what to say to him about their future sleeping arrangements, and at the same time feeling happy that he must care deeply for her, she decided to remain all business. "Point the gun down, Brad."

He sighed. "I was afraid he was going to shoot you."

She slipped into her shoes. "Yeah, well, he didn't, as you can plainly see."

"What's in the bag?"

"Take out." She handed him the doggie bag.

They started walking toward Dave's blown-up car. "So, what did you two talk about?"

"He thinks you're my lover."

"What did you say?"

"I told him I'd only sleep with you if he didn't die."

Brad's eyes lit up. "So he's going to give up, right?"

"He's going to die, Brad." She thought to put her hand in the crook of his arm, like lovers do, but then remembered all the lenses trained on them, so she interlocked her fingers behind her back and just walked beside him.

Behind them, Jerry secured his fortress for the night, dropped the steel panels and mercifully turned off *Anything Goes*, which everyone greatly appreciated.

When they got past the wall, she pulled Brad to a stop. "He's going to kill again, body count in the hundreds, but he says it'll be the last time. When the clock hits zero, he's going to tell me where the other bombs are placed, all disarmed but one."

"Just great. Did he say which one?"

"The hot one is the bomb he's planted here. However, it won't go off if I do everything he asked of me."

"What's the point?"

"Don't interfere with him. Don't let Bertrum get his grubby hands on anything. I know what he wants done, and if anything doesn't go as planned... Boom! His words exactly."

"Jesus."

"Talk to Bertrum. I've got to follow a lead." She strode off toward her Crown Vic.

"I'll go with you."

She stopped and turned around. "What don't you understand about *talk to Bertrum*? He's a loose cannon. I can't stand that guy. You stay here and keep a lid on him. I'll be back."

Joyce drove directly to her office. Sitting at her computer, she searched Alice Ann Hanson on yellow pages dot com. She got her last known address on South Owens Street in Lakewood, Colorado.

It was 9:00pm by the time she pulled up in front of the single story house set across the street from an old gated culvert barely visible in the haze of a faraway streetlight. The house lights were out, the lawn was overgrown, and the eves were rotted, giving the place a forlorn look of longing for better days gone by.

Sitting in the car, she imagined Brenda as a little girl, playing in the front yard surrounded by a white picket fence, now peeling with neglect. The windows emitted joyous light, and she could smell a home-cooked meal, hear the CBS Evening News on the TV, and see Jerry reclined in his recliner, a true king of his castle. Then the good life had turned on the whim of a drunken fool and left him a homicidal maniac.

Anything Goes

There were rows of homes a hundred yards to the east of the house and a golf course to the west, a stone's throw away. She imagined the serenity this place must've offered before civilization encroached.

Quietly, she got out of her car, reached for her purse, and left the keys in the ignition in case she had to beat a hasty retreat. The only sounds she heard, other than the noise her shoes made walking on the road, were crickets chirping and the babbling of Bear Creek.

She walked slowly around to the backyard and stumbled, causing her to break off her right high heel. "Shit." As it was now getting dark, she took out a government-issued FBI flashlight from her purse and moved on, limping and perturbed. She shined the beam on a small shed behind the main house then swept the ground for any more potholes. After walking up to the backdoor she tried turning the door knob. The door swung open as if the house was expecting her.

With her heartbeat rising faster, she stepped inside and made her way into the kitchen. Shining the light around, she saw the sink filled with dishes all strung together by cobwebs. In the living room, she swept the flashlight from side to side. Seeing a picture on the wall, she had to get closer to see through the dust. It was a picture of Jerry, Alice, Brenda, and Jerald taken when Brenda was only a child, maybe seven years old. She took it off the wall and set it on the dusty couch where she wiped it with the palm of her hand.

It's Jerry, all right.

The room lights blazed on, nearly binding her, and before she could scream, she saw Jerry leaning against the doorframe. He wore a long coat and hid his hands in the deep pockets, deep enough to hide a gun. "You can see it better with the lights on."

She dropped the flashlight next to the picture. "Are you going to kill me?"

"You have presented me with a problem, Joyce. What am I going to do with you for the next eighteen hours?"

"You could start by telling me what the hell is going on."

"I can't do that."

"Then let me walk out of here, no questions asked."

"I can't do that either. Brad will know that I was able to get out of my fortress."

"So you *can* be in two places at the same time. You killed that poor caretaker."

"I'll say this for you, Joycie. You turned out to be smarter than all the rest of them put together. I didn't put enough credence in your ability to figure me out. Perhaps I should say congratulations."

"That's not necessary. I've been trying to find a way to save your life. To do that, I have to know what makes you tick. That's what forensic psychiatrists do."

"Just like every other goddamned shrink, opening old wounds that are better left scarred over. Now what am I going to do?"

"Let me help you."

"Shut up. Let me think. I want you to call Brad on your cell phone and tell him you have a family emergency and that you'll contact him the day after tomorrow. Be brief."

"Brad isn't stupid."

"Then make your story believable."

She made the call. The line connected. "Brad—"

"Hey, babe. Want to get a little late dinner?"

"I can't." She breathed. "My sister is sick in Kansas City. I have to go home, but I should be back in two days."

"Oh, no. I hope it's not serious."

"It is serious. See you when I get back from Kansas. Bye."

She hung up and glared at Jerry. "Satisfied?"

"Now turn off the phone so it can't be tracked."

As she watched the display go black, she never felt more alone and helpless in her life.

#

Brad looked at Dave. "She said her sister is sick in Kansas City and she has to go home."

"That sucks. We need her here."

"But I don't think she has a sister. In fact, I swear she told me she grew up in Colorado Springs...an only child."

"Call her back."

Brad got a recording. *"This is Doctor Joyce Taylor...*

He hung up. "Shit, shit, shit! I don't like this, Dave."

"Maybe she's doing something for Jerry."

"I'm going to call that fucker right now."

#

Jerry was still leaning against the wall when his cell rang. "Don't make a sound unless you want Brad to be a widower before you become husband and wife." He answered, "Hey, Brad. I was just going to call you. When are your boys going to clean up that mess in my yard?"

"Have you talked to Joyce since this afternoon?"

"Oh, Joyce?" He sniffed. "Now, Brad. Did you two have a lovers' spat?"

"I asked you a question."

"And I'll answer it. No."

"No?"

"That's the answer, so now you say..?"

"Goddamn it. Do you know where she is?"

"Same answer, Brad. Now what do you say...?"

"Shit." He hated that condescending prick. "Thank you."

"There! Was that so fuckin' hard?"

"If anything happens to her—"

"Talk to you in the morning, Brad. Won't be long now and this will all come to an end."

Jerry shut off his cell phone and stood there in deep thought. Then: "I'll tell you what I'm *not* going to do, Joyce."

"You're not going to kill me...I hope."

"I'm not going to stop you from leaving, but if you do, I'll set off all my remaining nukes, and the deaths of at least a hundred thousand people will be on your shoulders, including Brad, Bertrum, and all the boys back home."

"You wouldn't."

"Think it over before you walk out of here. A hydrogen bomb is nothing to bet against."

Joyce thought it over and reluctantly agreed. "Now what?"

Jerry showed her Brenda's bedroom. "You can sleep here. Brenda wanted to be a psychiatrist one day, so she would be honored to have you stay in her room. Remember, if you have second thoughts and call Brad, I could be shot dead in a standoff and my blood pressure monitor will set off the nukes. I'll get my *Biblical pound of flesh,* one way or another."

Joyce lay in Brenda's bed all night and didn't sleep. She just hugged one of Brenda's old teddy bears.

Less than a mile away, Brad was not sleeping either. He was thinking about Joyce but not in a sexual way. He kept running the dilemma through his mind as to whether or not to call Joyce's parents in Kansas City or Colorado Springs in the morning, if he could find a listing for them.

There was no one for Jerry to call. He had already sent a

GO code to his computer using his cell phone. It was his failsafe system in case Joyce called Brad. He knew he could send the shutdown sequence in the morning...if all went well tonight. He got into his dusty bed for the first time since Alice died, and then reached over and patted his wife's old pillow. "I'll be joining you soon, honey." He turned out the light and dozed off into a cautious sleep—but not for long.

At 2:47am, Brad got an idea. He put in a call to Quantico communications. "I need the location of the last call I received from Doctor Joyce Taylor's cell phone."

"Twice in one day, Agent Tillman? Are you still having trouble with your girlfriend?"

"I wish it was that simple."

The FBI coordinated with the cell phone company and determined she'd called from a location about three-quarters of a mile south of him.

"Where is she right now?"

A moment later the agent replied. "Don't know. Either her phone is off or the battery is dead."

"Shit." He hung up, and breathing a sigh of relief, he figured she was probably on her way back here when she heard the news about her sister. Maybe she'd lied when she said she was an only child. But why would she do that? And why did she say her home was in Colorado Springs. Confusion and worry robbed him of his sleep all night.

Jerry was awake also. He sat in his living room, rocking back and forth and looking out the window into the darkness, his yard only illuminated by a faraway streetlight.

Joyce got up also and meandered into the living room, still holding the teddy bear. "May I join you?"

Jerry gave her permission in a calm but soft voice. "Sure, pull up a chair." As she sat in the nearby recliner, he added, "That was Alice's chair."

Joyce immediately stood again. "I'm so sorry. I didn't know."

"Sit down. I didn't mean you couldn't sit there. Now look out the window. You see that streetlight out there? Which way do you think it's pointing?"

Joyce studied the cone of light. "Maybe to the left?"

"No, it's to the right. It's an optical illusion. Alice and I used to joke about it...that maybe it moved back and forth. Those were good days. My son played high school football. He was a good young man. I remember the day he told us it was his duty to join the army. Now I think about all those young men who gave their lives for this shithole of a country. Politicians don't send their kids to war...just other people's kids."

"Old men make wars, young men fight them." She sighed. "It certainly isn't fair."

"The sun will be coming up soon on the day of retribution, and it'll be my last day on earth. I won't see the sun rise again. It'll be a good day."

"Jerry, it won't be a good day for your victims, will it?"

"Those sons of bitches are not victims. My son was a victim of government stupidity. My wife and daughter were victims of injustice. My only regret is that I don't have enough nukes to kill everyone in Washington."

"So you're saying there's a nuke in Washington?"

"Go back to bed, Joyce. You remind me of the daughter I lost. No harm will come to you. If only one person in my family had lived then maybe I could have withstood the grief."

"Don't turn your grief into revenge."

"It's too late."

Without another word, Joyce got up and went back to bed only to lay there and wait for the dawn.

At 8:25am, Jerry woke up to the sound of the garbage disposal running. Walking into the kitchen, he saw Joyce washing the five-year-old dirty dishes. "What the fuck are you doing?"

"The dishes are dirty."

"Stop. I want this house left the same way it was the day my wife and daughter died."

Joyce wiped her hands on a dusty towel. "Sorry."

"I'm glad you didn't call Brad."

"You left me no choice. Now I'm guilty of aiding and abetting. Isn't there anything I can say to stop you from killing again?"

"No! You could fix us some breakfast, though. There's plenty of canned food in the cabinet to your left. I think I'll go watch the news and see if we made the morning edition."

#

Back at Jerry's makeshift Alamo, from the house turned makeshift headquarters, Brad looked at the closed off balcony through binoculars. There was no sign of anything astir in the house. "Where the hell are you, Jerry?"

Bertrum walked up. "See anything?"

"I have a gut feeling he's not in there."

"Where do you think he is and how did he get out?"

Handing the binoculars to Bertrum, Brad shrugged. "If I knew that, it wouldn't be just a gut feeling."

Bertrum trained the binoculars on the digital clock. "Shit!"

"What's the matter?"

"The clock is counting down from three hours and fifteen minutes."

At almost the same moment, Brad's phone rang. It was Joyce, but before he could answer, she hung up. "Son of a bitch." He called her right back only to get her recording again.

"What's the problem," Bertrum asked.

"I know there's something wrong." Brad called Jerry.

"Good morning, Brad."

No Darth Vader voice? What the hell? The killer suddenly sounded human. "Come out on the balcony where I can see you while I talk to you."

"I'm not dressed."

"Five minutes then. I'll be standing by the Mercedes."

"Make it one hour. I have to do my hair."

"I said five minutes."

"Don't push your luck, Brad. I said one hour...or do I have to buy the time by blowing up another tourist attraction?"

"Okay. One fucking hour. If you're not on the balcony by then we'll storm the place with more firepower than Iwo Jima—"

"You're forgetting about the nukes, Brad. My blood pressure problem...remember? They'll all go *BOOM!*"

"Fuck."

"Relax, Brad. We'll be there."

Brad's face lost all expression. "What do you mean *we*?"

"Nothing. A simple slip of the tongue."

"Remember, Jerry, one hour."

He hung up on the persistent FBI fucker then grabbed Joyce by the arm. "Come on, kid. We're going for a walk."

"Wait a minute. I can't walk very well. My heel is broken."

"Then get a pair of shoes from Brenda's closet."

Jerry watched as Joyce picked through Brenda's shoes and put on a pair of flats that fit so-so. In the process, she clandestinely turned on her cell phone and left it on the closet floor. She stood and straightened her dress. "These will do."

"Let's go." He took her across the road to the culvert and unlocked the gate with a key he'd lifted from under a rock. "Keeps the kids and varmints out of my tunnel. Get in."

It was dark and dank and she didn't like this idea one bit, but knowing Jerry wouldn't harm her, she complied.

He locked the gate behind them. Then switching on a flashlight he'd stashed nearby, he shot the beam into the darkness that ran all the way to his fortress. "Be careful and walk only on the boards. I wouldn't want you to trip and break a leg. Brad would shoot me." Jerry took hold of her hand.

Joyce kept her eyes on the floorboards as she followed him, holding his hand all the way. The old runoff tunnel got damper and mustier, and the farther in they walked, the more the chill set into her bones. Neither of them said anything; the sound of dripping water was all that broke the silence.

The trip took about fifteen minutes. Jerry coaxed her up some makeshift steps to the Alamo's basement. When she saw a steel case with a glass top sitting on the cement floor, she let go of his hand. "That's the hydrogen bomb, isn't it?"

"'Fraid so, kid."

The chill she'd felt in the tunnel was a heat wave compared to the ice flowing in her blood right now. "Please, Jerry. Don't let that thing go off. It'll wipe out half of the Denver Metropolitan area."

"It won't go off, not necessarily anyway. It all depends on what happens in the next two hours."

The basement was cram-packed with canned food stored on shelves, and a huge chest freezer hummed along the far wall. She walked by a workbench and some tools. "Is this where you built the bombs?"

"I built them in the shed behind my house."

She remembered seeing it but had thought nothing of it.

They got to the second floor of the house just in time to hear Brad shouting into a bullhorn. "Come out on the balcony now or we storm the building. Trust me, Jerry...rubber bullets won't kill you but they'll make you wish you were dead."

Brad was about to issue the order to dynamite a hole in the first floor wall when the loud speakers blasted at ear splitting decibels:

Anything Goes

Anything Goes...

Still holding the bullhorn, Brad looked up to see a man staring down at him. No Darth Vader mask, but a white-haired guy wearing bifocals and sporting age spots on his forehead. "Brad," he shouted down in a smooth firm voice. "I'm here. You can call off your dogs."

"Turn off that fuckin' song. I can't get that tune out of my head. I hate it."

"Sorry, Brad, I can't hear you. The music must be too loud, so you're gonna have to shout. Now what can I do for you, Brad-o?"

"You can tell me what the fucking time on that clock means." It read: *1:59:32...31...30...*

"No can do, Brad. To use an old worn-out line, I could tell you but then I'd have to kill you. Joyce wouldn't like that, and to be honest, I wouldn't like it either. Why don't you and Joyce take the next two hours off and go on a picnic or to a motel and then report back here, and maybe we can get together for a really late lunch or early dinner. Your choice."

"Fuck you Jerry," Brad yelled. "We can't find Joyce."

"Whoa, Brad. Don't tell me she ran away." He laughed.

"Hey, everybody, the bride is AWOL."

Joyce wished she could call out to Brad, but she said nothing for fear he might go bananas and start shooting.

"Better go find her, Brad. She must be drowning in her tears."

"I'll be back, goddamn it."

"That's the spirit."

#

Back at the headquarters house, Brad asked the officer on duty, "Where's Bertrum."

"He had a funeral to go to, sir. He'll be back this afternoon."

Worrying over Joyce, Brad began checking on her story about her sister being sick. On the computer, he tapped into Kansas City voter registration files and came up blank. When he did the same for Colorado Springs, he found a listing for Mr. and Mrs. Taylor. He dialed the phone number on record.

"Hello," a woman's voice answered.

"This is Agent Brad Tillman from the FBI. Please excuse me for interrupting, but do you have a daughter named Joyce?"

"Oh my God, Joyce. Is she okay? Has something happened to her?"

"No, please, don't be alarmed. I just need to know... Does she have a sister in Kansas?"

"Oh, heavens, no. She's our only child."

Brad's heart slammed around in his chest like a caged animal. "Thank you for your time." He hung up. "Son of a bitch." Last night when Joyce called, she'd tried to tell him something was wrong...seriously wrong, but he was so stupid, he didn't get the memo. "Where the hell could she be?"

"Dear God," he prayed in desperation. "Please let her be all right."

#

Jerry closed the steel shutters to his balcony and turned to Joyce who was sitting at the table with a stoic look on her face.

"Nothing to do now but wait. Want to play some cards?" He dealt a hand of *Go Fish*.

"What are we waiting for, or is it still some guarded secret?"

"A funeral, Joyce." He looked over his cards. "Got any

threes?"

"Go fish."

"You'll know everything soon. I promise you."

#

Brad, while sitting in his car and eating leftover burnt meatloaf, received a call from Quantico. The agent told him, "Doctor Joyce Taylor's cell phone is active now."

"Where is it?"

"Same place the last call came from, which turns out to be on South Owens Street about three-quarter miles from you."

"Text me the coordinates."

Brad drove slowly down the street toward the GPS coordinates Quantico had sent him until he spotted Joyce's Crown Vic parked in front of an old house. He pulled up behind her car and, after taking out his 9mm Glock, slowly made his way to the driver's door. The keys were in the ignition but no sign of Joyce.

She must be in the house.

Gun low, he stalked to the front door. It was locked. He moved around back and tried that door. Unlocked. With both hands on his gun, he entered the backroom and swung his arms to and fro, pointing at everything. No one around. In the kitchen, he inspected an open can of raviolis. Smelled fresh. She was here not long ago, but something must've interrupted her meal.

He checked every room. One bedroom could have been a young girl's. The closet was open. Moving toward it gun first, he saw a cell phone on the floor surrounded by shoes. Someone wanted that phone found. He picked it up. Sure enough. It was Joyce's phone. But where was Joyce? "Shit." And why was she here? A wave of frigid desperation coursed through his body.

In the living room, he saw a blank place on the wall and found a picture setting on a dusty couch. It was a family portrait. A flashlight lay next to it: FBI government issued. Joyce's flashlight? He shined it on the portrait and immediately recognized the patriarch, white-haired Jerry Hanson.

"Son of a bitch." Joyce had found the fucker's real house. Heart racing with dread, he dialed Jerry.

#

Jerry laid down his cards. "Looks like your lover is calling." He answered the phone. "What's up, Brad?"

"I'm in your living room, Jerry, that's what's up. I know you've got her. Put Joyce on the phone right now."

"Fuck." Jerry swiped the cards off the table. "Looks like the gig is up, kid." He handed the phone to Joyce.

"I'm so sorry, Brad. I should've called you right away when I found his house. I'm so, so sorry."

"Are you all right?"

"He has a bomb in the basement. I think it's going to go off when the clock reaches zero. Get as far away as you can and forget about me." With that statement, Joyce began to cry profusely and clutched the phone to her breast. "I don't want to die, Jerry."

With a smirk on his face, he snatched the phone from her. "So, Brad, it seems that we have reached an impasse. You have my house and I have a very pretty but sad redhead with tears cutting little rivers through her makeup. So here's what we're going to do. You're going to drive up in my driveway and you're going to sit there; and in about five minutes, Joyce is going to come out and get in your car, and you're going to kiss her and say that all is forgiven. Got it, Brad?"

"Got it, Jerry."

Anything Goes

"Come on, Brad. What do you say to good-old Jerry?"

"I'm going to kill you."

"Nah, you know the drill by now. Two little words, Brad."

He exhaled in defeat. "Thank you."

"That's it. You're a winner. Five minutes, Brad. It's over for you and Joyce."

Jerry took her hand and kissed it. "This is really goodbye this time. Tell Brad he was a tenacious adversary and that I salute him. Go to your lover now, kid."

"He's not my lover. Come with me, Jerry."

He smiled. "I'm not into threesomes. Now go."

Joyce left the house and ran to Brad.

With Joyce now safely seated beside him he made a hasty U-turn exit out of the driveway and raced down the street. He drove about a mile down Morrison Road and then pulled over where he followed Jerry's instructions, kissing her first then: "All is forgiven."

"He thinks we're lovers," she whispered.

"Well, are we?"

"As long as he's alive, it's a possibility. And now I know his weak spot."

With lipstick on his mouth, he said, "You know how he gets back and forth."

"There's a tunnel." She smoothed the red on his upper lip.

"Show me."

Minutes later, Brad arrived at the gated culvert. They got out, and she showed him where Jerry hid the key.

Brad got Dave on the phone, and soon, Lakewood cops, SWAT, and FBI agents converged on the tunnel. Bertrum would miss all the action because he was at a funeral.

Joyce briefed the team. "The bomb is the basement at the end of the tunnel."

Dave asked for volunteers to go in and get it. "We can't stop him from setting off the nuke, but maybe we can move it to the south end of Chatfield State Park and evacuate everyone within a five mile radius."

Joyce thought to correct him, to order a fifteen mile radius, but what good would it do to panic the population? She had to believe that Jerry wouldn't detonate a hydrogen bomb.

"Any volunteers?" Brad asked. "Don't everyone speak up at once."

Anything Goes

Lt. Peterson stepped forward. "SWAT will do it."

"You and your boys go in first." Then Dave called his wife. "Peggy—"

"Dave, what's going on? It's all over the news. You're in a hostage standoff with a maniac who has a nuke? Are you in danger?"

"Peggy, I'm always in danger. Just got a little cut on my cheek is all. I'm fine. I'll be home soon."

"I love you."

"You too, and give my love to the kids." He hung up and turned to Peterson. "I'll go in with you."

An officer reported in. "We're cordoning off the area now, sir, five miles in all directions."

"Let's hope we won't keep folks out of their homes for very long."

"Yes, sir."

The bomb recovery team went in.

#

Brad and Joyce sat in his car and listened to the chatter on the police SWAT channel. Guilt for not telling him what she knew made her speak up now. "Five miles isn't enough."

"The nuke in Utah took out a two mile radius. If he made all the bombs the same, then yes—"

"He didn't, Brad. He made one different."

"Different how?"

"The bomb in the house is a hydrogen bomb."

Brad looked at her like she'd grown fangs. "You're fucking kidding me."

"Fifteen mile radius, incinerated, but I don't think it matters. He's not going to set it off."

"We can't evacuate the entire city. Hell, the fallout alone would make Colorado uninhabitable for decades."

"Just relax. Let Jerry play this out. I'm sure I know what makes him tick."

"You better be right."

"If I'm wrong, what difference does it make?"

He put his arm around her. "At least we're together."

Joyce examined her fingernails. "God forgive me, but I'm actually sorry Jerry's going to die today."

"He said that?"

"It's his death wish. I just wish I knew who he's going to kill before he kills himself."

#

Anything Goes

Dave and the SWAT team hurried down the tunnel, only to find an iron gate blocking their way to the basement. A bolt-cutter-proof lock the size of his fist secured the huge latch. "He must've known we'd be coming."

"We can still get in," Lt. Peterson told Dave. "But we can't do it quietly."

A sergeant came forward and pressed a glob of C-4 on the lock then stabbed it with a detonator. "Everybody back."

Bang!

They heard a single gunshot and ducked.

Dave realized it came from inside the house. "Blow it."

The C-4 went off with a quick boom, showering the team with dirt and dust. The lock was destroyed. Climbing into the basement, the recovery team found the bomb and quickly determined it was a fake, just like the other one from Plymouth Rock.

Dave led the others up to the next floor. He was the first to see the coffin. Carefully, he stalked to it, the barrel of his M-16 leading the way. After opening the lid, he stared in amazement at the corpse inside. It wasn't Jerry. This guy had been dead for a long time. The body was naked, freezing cold, and frost ringed a hole blown in his chest and traced incisions made by the coroner during an autopsy.

As he and the other SWAT team members looked at the frozen body in the coffin, the elevator door opened. Jumpy team members spun around and greeted it with a hail of SWAT team bullets. The elevator was empty.

"Jerry must want me to go upstairs." Dave got on the elevator and pushed the second floor button. As the elevator door closed, Dave took one last look at his friends and wondered if he would ever see them again.

The elevator stopped halfway up to the second floor. "Shit." In order to get out, he'd have to leave his weapon behind, a clever way for Jerry to disarm him. He opened the ceiling escape hatch and pulled himself up through the opening. The outer elevator doors on the second floor slowly started to open on their own. Dave cautiously peered into the room. He saw that it was empty so he climbed out of the elevator shaft and leaned against the wall. "Brad, do you read me?" he asked into his headset mike.

"What do ya got, Dave?"

"The place is empty. There's a body in the coffin, but he's not our guy, younger, maybe twenty five...thirty years old at most. He's been dead for months, looks like he took a shotgun blast to his chest. I think I've seen him somewhere before."

"The bomb recovery team says the nuke is a fake. That's a relief. Any sign of Jerry?"

"The rat has another hole to hide in. Do you and Joyce want to take a look at the corpse?"

"We're on our way."

Dave continued to check out the second floor. He sat down at the desk computer. A countdown clock on the screen showed *0:2:3...2...1... in bright red letters.*

The monitor came on with a video from Jerry.

"Hi, Dave. Find what you're looking for? Don't bother hunting for me. I'm long gone. Remember the old man with the walker you met when this all began? He just got a free ride from the Lakewood Police Department. I hope that cut on your cheek is healing nicely."

"Fuck." Dave paused the recording and radioed his men. "Anyone give a ride to an old man."

"I did, sir," came back.

"Is he with you now?"

"I dropped him at a bus stop. Should I go back and see if he's still there?"

"No, don't bother. He didn't get on the damn bus."

0:1:31...30...29...

Dave restarted the video.

"As you see, I left you a present in the coffin. I could help you identify him, but you should remember where you met the asshole."

Dave paused the recording and thought about the man in the coffin, came up blank. He turned when he heard the elevator start working. The door opened. Brad and Joyce stepped out. "Over here. Our boy is on the computer."

Brad and Joyce joined him.

0:1:04...03...02...

Dave restarted the video.

"I assume by now we are all together: Dave, Brad, and the vivacious and beautiful Joycie. You're probably wondering what comes next. Well, I'll tell you that the clue to my secret lies with the cocksucker in the coffin. I killed him three years ago, and today I'm going to wipe out his entire bloodline. I only have two nukes left, one for his family and a very powerful one for me."

Joyce gasped. "The hydrogen bomb."

"You know, a nuke can vaporize everything in close

range in approximately a millionth of a second. Not such a bad way to die, now is it? Beats being shot by a sniper or killed in a head-on car accident, aye? There's really no such thing as an accident when an alcoholic cocksucker is behind the wheel."

"His family was killed by a drunk driver," Joyce put in.

0:0:50...49...48...

"It's the ultimate tragedy. All your hopes and dreams are gone in an instant, and there's nothing left except memories for those left behind. Don't worry. I won't be bitching to you all much longer. As a matter of fact, you'll notice the countdown clock is at forty-five seconds. Do you know my wife and daughter believed in the trinity: the father, son, and Holy Ghost? I believe in a form of the trinity. Do you believe in the government's trinity, Brad?"

"Where's he going with this?" Brad asked over Dave's shoulder.

0:0:30...29...28...

"Congress, the Supreme Court, and the President, they're a trinity, wouldn't you say, Brad? But they believe our laws don't apply to them...only to all the poor bastards like you and me. One of them, who thought he was impervious to our laws, was a well known Senator from Wyoming. I enjoyed blowing the fucker's brains out."

"He was killed up in Casper," Brad chimed in. "The same night the caretaker was killed in the cemetery down here. We had no idea the cases were connected."

"Are these clues starting to refresh your memory, Dave? I'll give you another clue. There's something buried in the Senator's family plot, where the Senator is being buried right now, but it's not his fucking drunk-ass kid. I want you all to feel free to quote me on this: a Geiger counter, like superman, cannot see through lead. So if the secret service thinks they have checked the grounds of the cemetery and all is safe, well, they are fucking dead wrong. I doubt the President can run fast enough. Goodbye, Joycie."

The video flickered off.

Dave gasped. "It's gotta be a live bomb."

0:0:0...

Brad grabbed his phone, about to dial Quantico to send out an alert to Casper when the computer switched over to a Channel Eight *Breaking News* report.

A visibly upset news anchor said, "The President, two of his top Cabinet advisors, at least thirty members of the

House and Senate, along with four justices of the Supreme Court have been killed by a powerful nuclear blast in Casper, Wyoming, during the funeral of Senator John Nathan Gee who was murdered in a Holiday Inn restroom three days ago. This is all the news we have from the scene so far."

Brad dropped the phone. "We're too late."

A shaken Joyce fell back onto the couch. "My God, Jerry did it. If only I could have stopped him, but I wasn't a good enough psychiatrist to break through to him. It's my fault."

Brad sat down beside her. "No, it's not your fault. He planned his revenge years in advance."

Dave had it all figured out. "The body in the casket is John Nathan Gee Jr., the Senator's son. Jerry stored the corpse in a freezer all this time. I remember now. The kid was a drunk and totally worthless. After he killed a woman and child in a head-on crash, his father used his influence to get him off easy. Jerry Hanson took the law into his own hands and killed Gee Jr., and then somehow he'd gotten into the funeral home and replaced the corpse with a nuke, knowing he'd kill the Senator sometime in the future, and that his body would be buried next to his son."

Brad finished the diabolical tale. "Family attends the funeral. Boom. The bloodline is wiped out."

Joyce blinked away tears. "I'd say Jerry was a genius if he wasn't so evil."

Dave agreed. "He knew the Senator's funeral would draw a huge crowd of government officials, too, whom he blamed for starting two wars and getting his son killed."

"I don't know if any of you know this..." Brad picked up his dropped phone. "Bertrum was at the Senator's funeral. We lost him too."

"No telling how many other innocent people died with him." Dave turned off the computer. "All we know now is that Jerry is still out there somewhere, but we don't know what he'll do next."

Joyce shuddered. "I do. He's got one person left to kill. Himself. And he has one more nuke."

***

SEVEN HOURS AFTER THE catastrophe in Casper, Wyoming, while a grief-stricken nation mourned its losses, the stock market plummeted, and the world reeled in chaos, a stoic Jerry Hanson sat on the hood of his Corvette and watched the sun slowly go down behind the hills west of the old trinity site in New Mexico where the first atomic bomb was exploded in 1945.

He was listening to his iPod as it played *Anything Goes*:

...world's gone mad...

#

At 9:29pm, panic-stricken residents of Alamogordo, New Mexico, flooded 9-1-1 emergency call centers to report seeing a bright light boiling in the sky followed by a loud explosion.

Jerry had found his Valhalla.

George S. Naas

About the Author

George S. Naas is a long-time Colorado resident who owns Golden Publishing Company and writes in a variety of genres. He's an ancient history buff and a romantic at heart. When he's not writing or working, he enjoys bowling and cross-fit. He lives in Lakewood with his wife Dana.

Look for other novels by George S. Naas

Invasion of the Lesbian Zombies

Abused and humiliated by men, Brenda goes on a quest for beauty and revenge that leads to her death on an operating table in Haiti, but with the help of a Voodoo High Priestess and Loa the Lesbian Goddess of the Universe, she's brought back from the dead with a mission to empower all women, recruit other beauties into her lesbian sisterhood, and destroy the men who've done them wrong.

Buy from Amazon: https://www.amazon.com/dp/0692135642

Finding True Love at 35,000 Feet

Captain John Peterson, a battle-weary Army Ranger on his way home from Afghanistan, meets Emma Mansfield, an accomplished Doctor of Optometry, on a flight from Athens International Airport to the USA. Their attraction for each other is immediate, and they begin a courtship filled with fun and romance. However, tensions over an ex-boyfriend turned stalker and the ever-present demands of the military threaten to tear the two apart, and even though they manage to finally get married, everything changes when a soldier in John's old unit, inadvertently left behind, is captured by the Taliban. Duty compels John to mount a rescue mission and go back to war, leaving a pregnant Emma alone to worry about the fate of the soldier she loves.

Buy from Amazon: https://www.amazon.com/dp/B01FGUFCQ0

God's Assassin

This is the story of two brothers, Horus and Seth, both gods of ancient Egypt. Horus is an assassin for the Eternal, Lord of Hosts, killing evil people in the name of justice. Seth is the greatest evil the world has ever known. 3500 years ago, Horus, unwilling to kill his brother, imprisoned him in a tomb to save the world from his tyrannical rule. Now the walls are crumbling, and soon, good and evil will clash in the final battle of Armageddon. Caught in the middle is an American family who will play a vital role in the fate of the world.

Buy from Amazon: http://www.amazon.com/dp/B00COW2O3I

Charlie the Cherry
This is a children's (ages 4-6) picture book that tells the story of the trials and tribulations of the last cherry on the cherry tree and how his faith helps him to become a new cherry tree.

Buy from Amazon: https://www.amazon.com/dp/B0155R5IAE